Immersed In Pleasure /
Submit To Desire

Two novellas in one! In the first story, *Immersed In Pleasure*, the Manhattan Mermaids—all of whom are virgins—entertain wealthy, powerful men in an exclusive club called Fathoms. Derek Prince doesn't believe they really exist, until he meets the stunningly sensual Xenia. The attraction is mutual. Unfortunately, giving in to temptation means the end of her life at Fathoms.

And in *Submit To Desire*, Charlotte Brand is tired of dull boyfriends and boring sex. Kingsley Edge, who owns clubs rumored to supply more than just cocktails, seems just the man to revive her: intense, sophisticated…and looking for a submissive he can train for an elite client. Soon, they are engaged in a series of lessons that test her darkest desires….

The Original Sinners Pulp Library

Vintage paperback-inspired editions of Original Sinners erotic novels and novellas.

THE AUCTION

IMMERSED IN PLEASURE and

SUBMIT TO DESIRE

THE LAST GOOD KNIGHT

LITTLE RED RIDING CROP

MISCHIEF

THE MISTRESS FILES

IMMERSED IN PLEASURE/SUBMIT TO DESIRE

TIFFANY REISZ

8th Circle Press • Louisville, KY

CONTENTS

IMMERSED IN PLEASURE

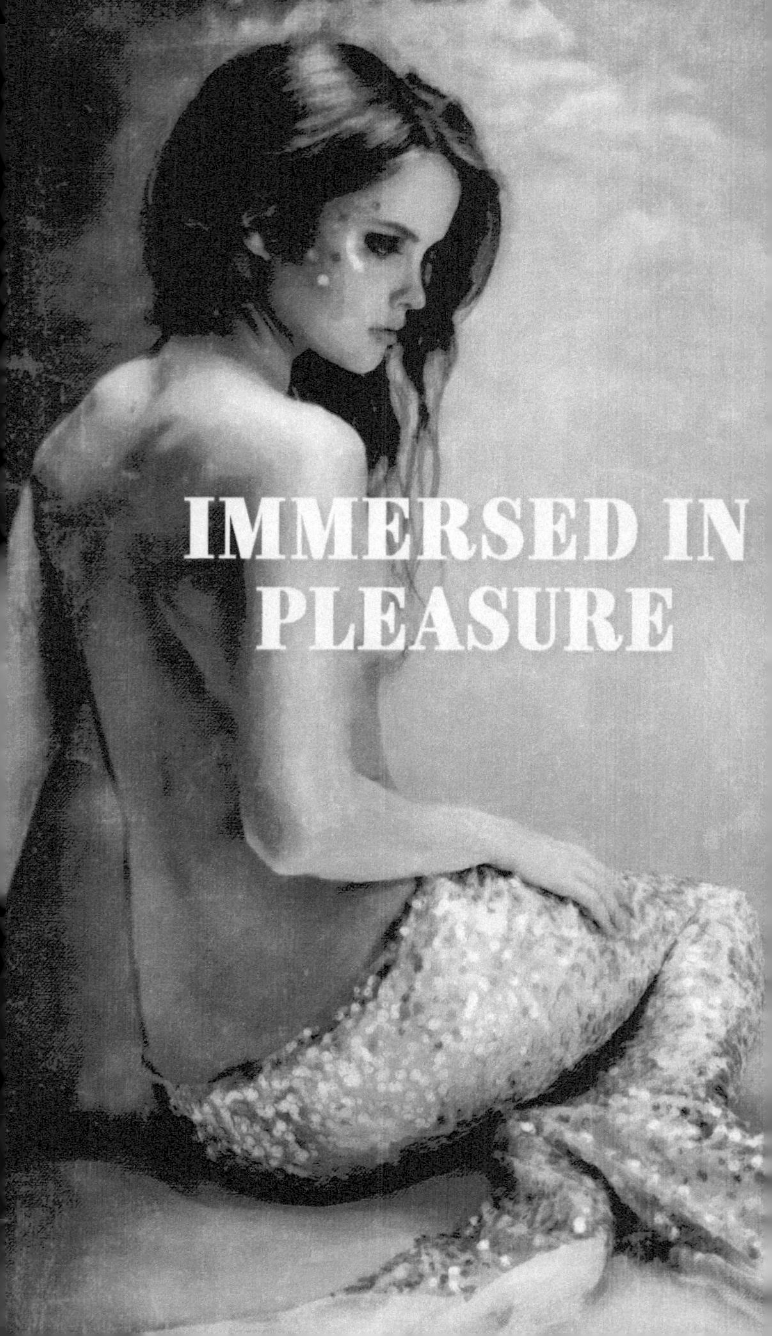
IMMERSED IN
PLEASURE

"I'm telling you, guys, they're mythical creatures. They're like, I don't know… unicorns or mermaids," Christian said.

At the mention of mermaids, Derek started paying attention to the conversation again. For the last five minutes, as Mark and Christian discussed their women troubles—specifically how many ex-boyfriends their current girlfriends had—Derek had tuned them out, his eyes fixed on an empty table across the nightclub.

"Oh, they're real." Derek raised his Old-Fashioned to his lips. "I knew one once."

"A virgin?" Mark asked. "A virgin over the age of twenty-one? I don't buy it. They don't exist."

Derek smiled into his drink. "Yes, she was a virgin," he said. "And a mermaid."

"Bullshit." Christian threw his napkin at Derek.

"No, he means it." Mark leaned back and gave Derek a long look. "Plus, he's the pretty one. If any of us were going to bag a virgin mermaid, it would be Derek Prince."

Derek half-laughed and rubbed his forehead. She'd called him pretty too. God, had it really been a whole year? He reached into his pocket and pulled something out. He didn't show it to Mark and Christian, merely weighed it in the palm of his hand briefly before tucking it into his pocket again.

"Believe it or not, it's true. And I saw her first right over there," he said, pointing to the table he'd been staring at a moment earlier.

"Over there?" Christian asked, a note of real concern in his voice. "At the VIP table? Kingsley Edge's table?"

Kingsley Edge, a wealthy half-French businessman of both renown and ill-repute, owned Cirque du Nuit, the club Derek, Mark, and Christian frequented at least once a week. According to rumor, a series of catacombs resided under Cirque du Nuit, catacombs that started under the club and stretched out underneath New York City like underground tentacles. Legend had it that all of Kingsley Edge's various clubs could be reached through the catacombs.

"Didn't know that then," Derek said. "It was a year ago. I was waiting for Ireland to show up—"

"Dude, I'm so glad you got rid of her," Mark interjected.

"And I saw this girl," Derek continued and felt his mind leaving the present and swimming back into the past. "This amazing girl with wet hair."

At his first glance of the girl, he thought she was one of those women who went bat-shit crazy with the hair gel. But when she moved, her hair moved with her. Not hair gel, just water. The white camisole she wore reached only to the bottom of her ribcage and had gone nearly transparent from the water in her hair. When she stepped into the blue light, he could just make out her pale pink nipples under the fabric. That alone would have held his attention all night except for one thing—she wasn't just wet and wearing transparent clothes, she was beautiful. Her dark brown hair hung in dripping ringlets over her face and down her back. She looked young, maybe only twenty or twenty-one, too young for this club anyway. Her large dark eyes and light-olive skin sported no makeup that he could discern. Watching her, he noticed she moved uneasily. A noise came from the edge of the club and she flinched, her eyes flashing wide open like a startled animal's. Twisting her hands together, she seemed uncomfortable in her surroundings and utterly out of her element.

Derek hadn't been able to take his eyes off her. Other than her little white camisole she wore a white skirt that rested low on her hips and revealed the full expanse of her flat stomach and lower back. The skirt clung tightly to her slim legs, all the way down to her ankles.

She must have sensed his gaze because she turned and stared back. Derek knew he shouldn't be staring, that he must seem like a psycho to her. But the look she returned wasn't angry, only inquisitive. Cocking her head to the side like a curious cat, she watched him watch her.

"So she was wearing all white and was wet from head to toe?" Christian asked.

Derek nodded. "I know. Sounds crazy, right? Gets crazier."

"What happened?"

"My table caught on fire," Derek said. "She saved me."

A man of about thirty-five with dark hair pulled back into a roguish ponytail sat with the girl. He wore a dark grey Victorian-era suit and riding boots. Derek rarely noticed other men, but he couldn't deny that the unusually handsome man the wet-haired girl sat with had an aura of power and mystery about him. The man snapped his fingers and the girl immediately turned her head to the sound. She drew close to him and the man whispered something in her ear.

Smiling, the girl pulled away. Derek's stomach tightened as she left the VIP area and walked gingerly down the steps, headed toward his table. In her skintight skirt she came to him, her steps nervous and delicate. As she walked, he noticed for the first time that she wore no shoes.

"Hello," Derek said as she sat across from him.

The girl stared at him for a moment. "Your table's on fire," she said.

Derek tried to discern if she was joking. He saw nothing in her eyes but innocent sincerity.

She pointed at his centerpiece. A black candle and a blue rose decorated every table in the club. His rose had dipped its head too near the flame and now quietly smoldered.

"Holy shit." Looking around wildly, he started to reach for his glass, but it contained an Old-Fashioned. Alcohol plus fire would equal a nightclub in ashes.

The girl laughed a soft tinkling laugh. Slowly she rose and leaned over the table. Taking her long brown hair into her hands, she twisted it, wringing just enough water out to douse the burning rose.

Because he didn't know what else to do, he laughed. "I'm glad this club has such gorgeous firemen on duty."

She ran her hands through her wet hair and separated it into three sections. "I'm not a fireman," she said, humming as she braided her long hair with nimble fingers.

"What are you then?"

"A mermaid."

She stretched out her leg toward him. Derek didn't know what he was supposed to be looking at but then he saw them. At first he thought her feet sported silver foot jewelry of some kind. But no, metallic silver tattoos of fins adorned the tops of her small, pale feet.

"No way," Mark interrupted. "She was one of *those* mermaids?"

"She was," Derek said, taking a sip of his drink. "I didn't think they were real either. Not until that night."

The Manhattan Mermaids. Believed to be the most beautiful women in the city, they entertained the wealthiest, most powerful men in the world. Kingsley Edge didn't just own Cirque du Nuit. He owned four or five other clubs, some of them so secretive they didn't even have names. One of the most exclusive was known as Fathoms. Fathoms supposedly had the usual sort of chic-chic nightclub stuff —cocktail waitresses, ridiculously opulent decor. But in addition to that, Fathoms had one thing no other club in the city had—mermaids. One could tell a mermaid if you met her on the street by two things, Derek had heard —they wore little silver mermaid pendants around their necks, and they had silver and blue metallic tattoos on their feet and ankles. Derek looked the girl up and down—check and check.

"You're a real mermaid?"

She gave him a mischievous grin. "Come find out."

Just then, Ireland decided to make her appearance—an hour late. For almost the entire hour, he'd been desperate for her to show up. Now that he saw her breezing through the door and heading his way, he fervently wished he'd been stood up.

"I can't," he said.

The tiniest glint of disappointment shone in the girl's midnight blue eyes. In such an open innocent face, the sadness rebuked him. He felt as if he'd knocked a baseball through a stained-glass window.

"Then goodbye," she sighed. "I'll never see you again."

She said the words with such earnestness that Derek knew he would be the idiot of the century to miss this chance. It wasn't only that The Manhattan Mermaids were so legendary that he still couldn't quite believe he'd been talking to one. It was her—this girl—not the rumors and legends who'd gotten to him. She'd saved his life…or at the very least his centerpiece. And she had such an innocence about her. He didn't meet innocent people in his line of work. As a defense attorney, he was often called a shark. He briefly wondered if sharks and mermaids were natural enemies or allies.

As Ireland reached the table, Derek made up his mind.

"You're late," he said.

"Couldn't remember if we were meeting at nine or ten," she said, shrugging. He couldn't recall just then why they were dating. Brainy and beautiful with her white-blond hair and her legs that went on for eternity, Ireland was fantastic in bed and—unlike his ex-wife— wasn't afraid to try anything. But she could also be cold and arrogant when she wanted to be. Tonight, she apparently wanted to be.

"We'll meet at your place at eleven and then I'll be an hour late." He stood up. "See you at midnight."

"Wait, where the hell are you going?" Ireland demanded. "I just got here."

"And I'm just leaving."

Derek raced to the VIP table and found it depressingly empty. His mermaid and the dark-haired man had vanished. The only sign the girl had even been there was a small puddle of water on the floor by the chair she'd been sitting in.

Water…. Derek stopped looking around and started looking down. Not far from the VIP table he found the watery outline of a bare footprint on the floor. A few feet further, he saw another tiny puddle of water glinting on the shiny dark blue tile. The drops led to a door tucked in a corner.

A metal EMPLOYEES ONLY sign decorated the door and gave Derek pause. In a club owned by Kingsley Edge, breaking the rules led to unpleasant consequences. But he'd abandoned one of the sexiest women in New York at his table for this chance, and he wasn't going to miss it.

He threw open the door and found a stair-well. Racing down the stairs, he prayed the water on the floor had come from her and not some clumsy waitress. At the landing two levels below Cirque du Nuit, he knew he was on the right track. Breathing in, he inhaled warm wet air scented with a trace of chlorine. He passed through another door and stopped immediately when he discovered he wasn't in Cirque du Nuit anymore or even the club's basement.

He was in Fathoms.

LOOKING around the dimly lit club, Derek couldn't believe the legend was true. The underground catacombs did connect all of Kingsley Edge's clubs.

Derek hid behind a column and studied his surroundings. The club had dozens of interconnected swimming pools scattered about the large room. Between and about them sat tables and chairs — chairs occupied by the highest of high society. Derek recognized several faces — with a real estate mogul for a mother and the deputy mayor for a father, Derek could recognize the wealthy and famous on sight. And everywhere he looked he spied money and power.

At the center of the room stood a two-story high transparent column about twelve feet across. In it swam a girl completely naked but for a silver belly chain. The silver fins tattooed on her feet, ankles and thighs glinted in the light. He tore his eyes from the column to another corner of the room. Another girl equally beautiful and equally naked, sat on a large rock at the edge of one of the pools. A man Derek recognized as a city councilman said something to the girl. She rolled her eyes and splashed water in his face. The gesture made the man laugh as if it was some sort of honor to be splashed by such a woman.

Derek tore his eyes from the scene and searched the club for his mermaid. Looking up, he saw a metal walkway at the top of the large column and a flash of white skirt. He found a staircase behind him, and at the top of the staircase he came suddenly face to face with his mermaid.

"Hello," she said, standing in a private alcove next to the top of the central swimming pool. "I thought I would never see you again."

"I forgot to thank you for putting out my fire," he said, wincing at how stupid he sounded.

She ran her fingers through her hair,

freeing it from its braid. "I'm waiting," she said, humming.

"For…."

"For you to thank me. You said you forgot to."

Derek shook his head. "Right. Thank you for putting out my fire. I didn't mean to stare at you upstairs. I've never seen a mermaid before."

"I stared back," she said simply.

"You did. Why?"

"I like your face."

"You like my face?"

"I do. It's pretty. But not girl pretty. Handsome prince pretty. And you have hair that's wavy like water. Even your eyes are water-colored, and your shirt. I probably thought you were a merman."

Derek looked down. He wore black slacks and a black vest over his French blue Oxford shirt. A little too GQ for him, he only wore these clothes because Ireland liked them so much.

"I'm not a merman. But I am a prince. Derek Prince," he said and held out his hand to her.

"Xenia." She ignored his hand and instead leaned forward to kiss him on the cheek. He shivered as her warm soft lips pressed into his cheek. "I have to go now, but you can stay if you like."

"Go where?"

"Underwater."

At that Xenia took a step back and pulled her camisole off. Her skirt came off next, and she stood before him completely naked.

Derek felt his eyes go as wide as hers. Although a sight to behold, the club paled before Xenia's naked flesh. Thin but with soft girlish curves, Xenia barely looked human to him. The silver metallic scale tattoos graced not only her feet and calves but the sides of her thighs and the edge of her hips. Her breasts, the perfect size, appeared designed to rest in the palm of his hand. A healthy red-blooded man, he couldn't help but stare at her breasts and between her legs. Completely smooth and hairless she seemed a being of eternal youth. His body tensed at the sight of such pristine flesh so unashamedly on display.

The girl, Xenia, reached for a silver chain and fastened it around her stomach. Little silver scales hung off it and dangled around her hips. She clasped silver bracelets on each wrist and connected them to the silver rings on her fingers. Around her forehead went a heavier silver chain like a small circlet. The body jewelry shimmered in the low light and rendered Xenia a creature of ethereal beauty.

She strode to the edge of the tall pool and dove gracefully into it. Derek ran back down the stairs and up to the side of the column. Around and around she swam, her long brown hair flowing behind her. She spun in slow graceful circles, arched under and around, and seemed to need almost no air. Derek watched her, unable to look at anything else. She swam to the edge of the column and smiled at him through the water. He pressed his hand to the glass and she laid her hand against the inside to meet his. But she pulled back quickly and swam off again.

"Ahh…that little one. She may be my favorite," said a lightly accented man's voice from behind him. Derek turned around and saw the man from Cirque du Nuit, the one in the Victorian suit and the ponytail standing behind him with a cocktail in his hand.

"She's amazing," Derek agreed. "She's the most beautiful girl I've ever seen in my life."

"*Merci.* I found her myself."

Derek stared at the man. *Merci,* he'd said. *Found her…*

"Oh my God. You're Kingsley Edge,"

Derek said. "I'm sorry. I didn't mean to barge into your club. She told me I should—"

The man shook his finger and tsk-tsked him in a manner that was infuriatingly French. "I know who you are, Mr. Prince. And I know who your parents are. Consider yourself on the guest list."

Derek followed Kingsley to the bar. They sat on stools side by side and said nothing until the bartender—a beautiful young blonde woman wearing a shimmering sea-green dress—brought them both fresh drinks.

"Ah, Urs," Kingsley said to the bartender as he took a drink of his Sidecar. "You are too good to me."

"Nothing's too good for our King." She leaned up to kiss him on the cheek as Xenia had to Derek.

"So you really are Kingsley Edge?" Derek asked. While Kingsley Edge's clubs were famous, the man himself was infamous.

Kingsley shrugged, a small smile playing over his lips. "It's a living."

"A very good one. My God, these girls are incredible." Derek counted at least a dozen stunningly beautiful naked girls swimming about the club or lounging on large rocks with their decorated feet tucked to the side. Not even the mermaids of lore could be more spectacular than the ones right in front of him.

"Incredible, yes. In many ways," Kingsley agreed. "My mermaids are my pride and joy. I went to Japan ten years ago and met a geisha. Such a woman I'd never seen before. How she talked and teased and entertained us all. I recall thinking the world needed more women like that—beautiful, mysterious, untouchable."

"Untouchable?" Derek asked. He glanced at Xenia, who continued to swim languid graceful arcs in the transparent column.

"*Oui,*" Kingsley said. "Untouchable…untouched. This is no gentlemen's club or brothel. If you're here for a lap dance, you're in the wrong place. All my mermaids are virgins."

Derek nearly spat his drink out. "Virgins?"

"*Bien sur.* Those who come here wish to see something truly unusual, something magical or mythical. Beautiful women, naked, exquisite, and all virginal."

"Even Xenia?" Derek asked.

"Even she."

"But she must be in her twenties, right?"

"She is. She started here at age eighteen and has been a mermaid three years now. I saw in the paper a little article about a girl who'd broken a record for holding her breath underwater. I met her the next week, and she's been here ever since."

"But that's crazy," Derek protested. "Why would women this gorgeous choose—"

"If I offered you an extraordinary sum of money to go a year without sex, would you do it?"

Derek stared at Kingsley and burst into laughter. "So it's the opposite of prostitution here?"

"I pay them to *not* have sex. As long as they stay intact, they can work very few hours, meet the wealthiest and most powerful men in the world, and leave whenever they wish. Most depart after a year or two with a rich boyfriend, a very large bank account, or both. Many, like Xenia, stay longer."

Just then a redheaded mermaid slid off her rock and dove back into the water.

"Come back, Alanna," the man at the table called after her. "Please?"

"No, go away," the girl, Alanna, said when she surfaced, "I don't like your tie. It's ugly."

Kingsley chuckled softly at the scene. "Mermaids," he said to Derek, "have cold hearts. To win the heart of one takes much perseverance."

Shaking his head, Derek could only gaze around him in awe. He understood it all now. Beautiful virginal women who were trained to be unimpressed by the wealth and power that surrounded them…no wonder this club attracted such a high caliber clientele. Seducing a stripper was child's play. But netting a virginal mermaid? Now that was a feat.

"But how do you know they're virgins?" Derek asked. "Can't they sneak out and do whatever they want?"

"We have ways of knowing." Kingsley took another sip of his drink.

"What ways?" Derek studied him out of the corner of his eye.

Kingsley merely swirled the ice in his cocktail. "Land is grand, Mr. Prince, but wetter is better. Some days, it is good to be the King."

At that, Kingsley strode off and sat next to someone Derek recognized as the top prosecutor in the state of New York. Glancing up, he saw Xenia swimming to the top of the column of water. Derek headed up the stairs again and found her just as she pulled herself from the water.

"You stayed," she said, smiling as she stood naked and dripping in front of him. She didn't reach for one of the dozens of towels stacked nearby. Nothing in her posture or manner seemed remotely seductive. Although everything in him longed to lick the water off her extraordinary curves, she appeared almost unaware of her naked body and the effect it had on him.

"I did stay. But I have to go now. Can I see you again?"

"If you come back, you can see me again. If you don't come back, you can't."

"Then I'll come back. I'll definitely come back."

"But go away now," she said as she started to walk off. "I like your face enough I want to know how it feels to miss it."

Grinning ear to ear, Derek nodded. He never knew getting dismissed could feel so good.

He returned to the club upstairs and found Ireland long gone. But he had told her he'd see her at her place. Even if she couldn't keep a promise, he could.

HE REACHED Ireland's apartment by eleven o'clock. Knocking on the door just before eleven, he half-hoped Ireland wouldn't answer.

For a month now, he'd been putting off the big "this isn't working" talk. They weren't exclusive. Whenever he started to consider it, she'd shift into bitch overdrive and all thoughts of happily-ever-after would go screaming out the window.

Ireland answered the door wearing only a white shirt—one of his—and wet hair. She always took a long hot shower when angry. Not a good sign.

"Can't believe you showed up." She stepped back to let him in.

"Told you I would. I'm even early."

Derek entered and sat on her couch. He hated how attractive she looked with her hair down and wet. Apparently, he'd acquired a wet hair fetish in only one evening.

Ireland exhaled heavily as she came to stand in front of him. "Derek, I'm sorry. It was wrong of me to be so late and not call. Forgive me?"

Derek shook his head and groaned. He hated these conversations. "Ireland, you're smart and beautiful and…." he began and discovered he'd already run out of compliments. "That's fantastic. But all you and I ever do is fuck or fight. If we're not doing one, we're doing the other."

"So?"

"So that's hardly a relationship. Look —" he began and she stopped him with a finger over his lips.

"So...." she said as she straddled his lap, a knee on either side of his thighs, "I'm done fighting."

"Ireland, not tonight. We have to talk —"

Ireland raised her hand and unbuttoned the top button of her shirt.

"Don't, Ireland."

She unbuttoned her shirt all the way to the bottom and let it slide off her arms and slip to the floor. She dipped her head and kissed his neck, his earlobe.

Against his will, Derek's body began to respond to her expert touch. She brought her breasts to his face and Derek suckled lightly on her nipples as she reached down and freed him from his pants. As he kissed her breasts hungrily, she rose up and pushed him inside her.

"Ireland, stop," he said as he tore his mouth from her body.

"Stop what? Stop this?" She moved her hips forward, taking him even deeper into her. Rocking against him, Ireland unbuttoned his vest and shirt and pushed them back. Running her hands down his strong chest, she pressed her hands into the hard flat plane of his stomach. Derek breathed in hard and hated himself for letting her have such power over him. Ireland used sex as a weapon. She wielded it like a trained assassin.

Leaning in close, Ireland let her hair tickle his bare shoulders.

The touch of her wet hair on his skin proved too much for him. He ordered her up and bent her over the back of the couch. Gripping her shoulders, he brutally drove into her. Her hips bucked frantically against his. She loved it rough, but tonight his force was for his benefit, not hers. With bitter, angry thrusts he slammed into her as she panted his name. He pushed into her so deep she flinched. All the water in the ocean couldn't put out the fire in his blood tonight.

Under him, Ireland groaned and gasped. Derek suspected half of Ireland's vocal pleasure constituted mere theatrics designed to keep him ensnared to her. Her orgasm seemed louder than usual, and out of spite Derek came silently. He pulled out of her as soon as he'd finished.

"See?" Ireland grabbed her shirt off the floor. "We're good together."

Angry with himself for letting her win again, Derek shoved his shirt back into his pants. "We're only good together when we're in bed."

"That was the couch," she said with an arrogant toss of her hair.

"And it wasn't good. It might have felt good but it wasn't good."

"Derek, what's your problem? You're hot and rich. So am I. You said yourself you weren't planning on ever getting married again. God knows I don't want a husband and a bunch of screaming brats around puking on my carpet and throwing cereal in my Porsche. We're right for each other. We make sense."

"We make nothing." Derek hastily buttoned his vest. He hated who he turned into around Ireland. "We don't even make love. I feel nothing with you. Tonight this girl kissed me on the cheek, and I felt more from that than I did five minutes ago when I was rammed up in you."

"What are you saying?" For a moment Ireland seemed almost human.

What was he saying? In those few brief moments with Xenia, he'd laughed, mostly at himself. He'd felt like an idiot, like a teenager, like a man on a mission—things he never felt with Ireland, things he never even felt with his ex-wife. "I'm sorry, Ireland. I want more."

The tiny moment of humanity had been an act. All the way to the door, Ireland pelted him with insults and profanities. Derek didn't respond. He merely walked out, found his car, and headed to his own apartment. On his way there, his mind kept returning to Xenia. Derek Prince—son of the deputy mayor of New York, partner in his own law firm by age thirty—and now he couldn't stop grinning at the thought of a twenty-one-year-old virgin who worked in a nightclub. Mark and Christian would die laughing if he told them. Then and there, he decided he would keep it to himself.

"Asshole," Mark interjected. "You could have told us."

"Seriously," Derek said, "I shouldn't even be telling you this much now. Nobody wants to get on Kingsley Edge's shit list."

"Bad list to be on, I hear," Christian agreed.

"Look, do you want to hear the story or not?" Derek demanded.

"Does it get better? The only sex in it so far is with Ireland, and even then you left the good parts out."

"There were no good parts with Ireland.

But yes, it gets better. And weirder. And yeah, there's definitely more sex."

⁂

THE DAY AFTER MEETING XENIA, his concentration at work had been shot. The hours crawled by. When the sun finally set, he wrapped up work earlier than usual. He showered, changed into black slacks and a black button-down. At eleven o'clock, he returned to Cirque du Nuit and headed straight for the stairwell.

Finding a seat at the lavish bar inside Fathoms, Derek ordered a drink and toyed with it as he kept an eye out for Xenia. Finally, he saw her slip out of one of the smaller pools and position herself on a rock next to a table. He could only stare at her glistening body as she tucked her silvery feet to the side and chatted with one of Fathoms's many preposterously wealthy patrons.

He tried to catch her eye but had no luck. Almost despairing of his inability to talk to her, Derek debated whether he should leave or stay.

"Welcome back, *Monsieur* Prince."

Derek turned around and saw Kingsley

standing behind him. Tonight he wore a slightly more modern suit—black Armani— and his hair down instead of back in last night's ponytail. A well-named man, he looked both aristocratic and undeniably edgy.

"Mr. Edge, Xenia asked me to come back. That's allowed, isn't it? I just want to talk to her."

"Of course. My mermaids are employees here, not prisoners. They see whomever they desire. Xenia asked me to give you this note." Kingsley handed him a piece of sea-blue paper covered in water splotches.

"A note?"

"You should feel quite flattered. I do not deign to play messenger often. Lucky for you, I'm in a very good mood."

"Do I want to know why?" Derek asked as he carefully unfolded the waterlogged piece of blue stationery Kingsley had given him.

"See her?" Kingsley pointed at a beautiful mermaid with long black hair, voluptuous breasts, and a wide bright smile. "My Emelia…this is her last night. Joining the Peace Corps or some other such nonsense." He said "nonsense," but Derek heard pride in his voice.

"And that puts you in a good mood?"

"Let's just say that, at her request, she will be getting quite a special send-off."

Derek could only imagine what he meant by that. He tilted Xenia's note into the light and read what he could of the wet words.

Hello my Handsome Derek Prince – If you stay until midnight I might turn into a pumpkin again. Wait, that's the wrong story, isn't it? I like how tall you are and that you smile when you look at me even when you think I can't see you.

"She likes you," Kingsley said.

"I like her. But we haven't gotten to talk much."

"She's a delight. Intelligent, unusual, and, of course, quite beautiful. I worry about her though."

"Why? She's amazing."

"She's been here so long, I fear she may have forgotten what the sun looks like. Perhaps you could remind her."

"I can do that. Happily. Pumpkin at midnight?"

"When she's finished for the night. There's a lounge upstairs and to the left. You may wait there if you promise that what you see tonight, you will not share with others. I'm very protective of my mermaids."

❧

AFTER PLEDGING HIS SILENCE, Derek headed up the stairs Kingsley had indicated. Taking a hard left down a tiled corridor, Derek found the softly lit and luxurious lounge empty of men or mermaids. Impatient for midnight and his chance to talk to Xenia again, Derek wandered around the lounge and out into the hallway. Across from the lounge, Derek found another room, this one appointed like a tasteful massage studio complete with padded table and bottles of exotic oils. Alanna, the redheaded mermaid from last night, stepped past him wearing only a towel. Without even waiting for him to look away, she dropped her towel and lay prone on the table. An attractive young man of about twenty-seven or eight followed her into the room and washed his hands. He poured clear thick oil into his hands and ran it through the mermaid's lustrous long hair. Then he doused the naked girl in a thick layer of golden oil and began to massage it into her skin.

The girl and her masseur chatted softly

during her massage. At one point, she flipped over to allow him access to the front of her body. She didn't seem the least fazed when he oiled her breasts and thighs. Daily hot oil massages as a perk of the job…no wonder Xenia didn't want to leave this place. Derek decided that massages might be something he'd have to implement at his law office. Maybe Christian and Mark would pull their weight a little more with that incentive.

"Dude, the commentary is not appreciated," Christian interrupted.

"But yes, massages at work," Mark agreed. "Now continue."

At first Derek thought it was an ordinary massage. With all the time the women spent in the water, Derek imagined they'd require an intensive skin-care regimen. But soon the rather perfunctory massage turned intimate as the masseur pushed apart Alanna's legs and rubbed high on her inner thighs. Sighing blissfully, she opened her legs even wider. The young man reached between her thighs and spread apart the folds of her vagina.

"You're shitting us," Mark breathed, his eyes going wide enough Derek had to laugh. "Hymen check?"

"Exactly," Derek said, flushing a little at

the intensity of the memory. "But not just that."

The man moved his fingers higher and began tracing tight circles around the mermaid's clitoris. She closed her eyes, raised her hips slightly and after a few minutes of the masseur's ministrations, she came with a flinch and a gasp. At no point during the procedure had he penetrated her in any way. Yet the look on her face indicated a very happy mermaid who'd just had a spectacularly strong orgasm.

"We can include that in our office massages." Mark took a fresh drink from their scantily-clad waitress. Derek knew Mark and Christian must be engrossed in his story as neither of them even bothered to flirt with her. "That won't be an HR nightmare at all."

"Screw our law firm." Christian collapsed back into his seat as if spent. "I'm going to find that guy and take his job. Massages with happy endings. Awesome."

Alanna, rolled off the table, picked up her towel, and strolled out of the studio. On her way out, she patted Derek on the cheek and kept walking. Just another day at the office.

"I guess swimming naked around the upper echelons of New York high society makes for some seriously immodest virgins," Christian surmised.

Derek shook his head, still unable to believe that he'd seen what he'd seen last year at Fathoms. "You haven't heard anything yet," he said, and took a deep breath before diving back into his story.

Intending to head back to the lounge, or maybe the men's room first and then the lounge, Derek turned around and came face to face with the striking blonde bartender from last night.

She arched her eyebrow at him. "Enjoy the show?"

Blushing guiltily, Derek knew he had no excuse for watching other than no one told him he couldn't.

"I'm sorry. Urs, right? That's your name?" The girl didn't bat an eyelash. "I was waiting on Xenia. Kingsley told me I could come up here."

The girl's anger flickered only slightly at the mention of Kingsley's name. "Xenia's happy here. This is her home. This place may seem like a freak show to you, but it's heaven here. Kingsley takes amazing care of his employees. The mermaids make incredible money, live in gorgeous *free* apartments, and as you saw, we get great benefits."

"Kingsley said Xenia's been here for three years. Don't you think she might want to have a relationship with someone eventually?"

"With someone who will see her as some kind of prize, use her, and then drop her when the shine wears off? When he realizes she's just a tattooed girl who had a very cool job once upon a time but now is as human as he is? That kind of relationship?"

"No. A real relationship. Marriage maybe, or kids. Or if not that, then at least a healthy sexual relationship with someone she's in love with. Is she going to be doing this when she's sixty?"

"You'll still want her when she's sixty?"

"I just want to get to know her. She's weird and beautiful, and I can't stop thinking about her. And no, I wasn't just thinking about having sex with her. Believe it or not, I'd really like to take her to lunch and talk. Is that so horrible?"

"It's not horrible, no," she said, the venom gone from her tone and profound regret in its place. "But this is better. Trust me."

Derek didn't know what to say. He glanced down at the floor and saw a flash of a silver tattoo on Urs's ankle. "You used to be a mermaid?" he asked, understanding her bitterness now.

"I did. But I was stupid and left."

"What happened?"

"Some rich pretty-boy jackass—sound familiar?—made me an offer I couldn't refuse."

"And?"

Urs started to walk down the hall. "I didn't refuse it."

⁂

DEREK RETURNED TO THE LOUNGE, Urs's angry words echoing in his ears. Maybe she had a point. If Xenia was happy here at Fathoms, why leave it behind for the uncertainty that came standard with the real world and real relationships?

"Hello, my Handsome Derek," he heard a voice over his shoulder.

He turned his head and found Xenia, naked and dripping, standing in the doorway to the lounge. Water droplets gleamed on her breasts and belly.

"I'm sorry. I think I've forgotten English," Derek said, blinking at her.

"It's cute how you can't stop staring at my breasts."

"Cute is better than sociopathic. I really do know what your face looks like."

"Really?" She put her hands on her hips. "Close your eyes."

Derek took a nervous breath and obeyed. He heard soft wet footsteps on the tile floor coming closer to him.

"Now," Xenia said, "Tell me what color my eyes are."

Derek smiled. "Dark blue like the ocean at night. And you have dark eyelashes that make them look ever bluer."

"Very good. You can open—" she began, but Derek wasn't finished.

"You've got a freckle under your left eye and another freckle on your bottom lip. It looks like a tiny smudge of lipstick and I'm dying to kiss it. You also have a birthmark on your derriere that I also wouldn't mind kissing."

Christian burst into slightly drunken laughter. "Did you really say 'derriere'?" he asked.

"I was trying to make her laugh."

"Did she laugh?" Mark asked.

"Better," Derek said.

With his eyes closed, he had tried to think of a few more lines to throw at her—how her hair looked like a silk veil as it trailed her in the water, how her nose crinkled when she giggled…but before he could get the words out, her lips, moist and cool, pressed against his lips, warm and ready. He expected a quick kiss, sweet and brief. But she surprised him again by turning her head and touching his bottom lip with her tongue.

Nearly groaning from the need to wrap his arms around her naked body and drag her to him, Derek forced himself to focus only on her mouth.

Soft and full, her lips moved on his with as much curiosity as hunger. She tasted clean and pure like water. He wanted to drink her.

Finally, she pulled back and Derek opened his eyes. She smiled down at him and he decided then and there that when he died, he would be buried at sea.

"You're an idiot, Derek," Christian said.

"I'm not arguing with that," Derek said. "But I was an idiot in love."

"What happened after the awesome kiss?" Mark asked.

"Nothing torrid," Derek said and saw Mark and Christian's faces fall like two kids who didn't get what they wanted for Christmas. "Not yet anyway." Their faces lit up again. "Unfortunately she put on clothes."

"What was she wearing?" Mark asked. "That hot white skirt and cami mermaidy thing again?"

"Pajamas. White shorts, a white tank top, white socks. She looked adorable."

"I want a mermaid," Mark sighed.

"I want torrid," Christian said and waved at Derek to go on.

"Torrid did happen that night. But not between Xenia and me." Their eyebrows raised. "It's about to get even weirder. And hotter."

Derek narrowed his eyes at Xenia. "Do you have any eights?"

Xenia bit her bottom lip, smiled, and shook her head. "Go fish."

"Dammit. I think you've rigged this game." Derek reached into the ocean to take a card.

"I'm even better at Old Maid." Xenia winked at him.

Derek laughed, relieved she had a sense of humor about her virginity.

"But Go Fish is my favorite," she continued. "Mermaids and fish are very good friends. I have connections."

Smiling, Derek sorted the cards in his

hand. This might go down in history as his oddest first date ever. In some respects, the date progressed very well—already he'd achieved access to Xenia's bed. But in other respects, he imagined his friends scoffing at his current activity. He and Xenia sat cross-legged on her covers, a deck of cards between them as they played Go Fish and talked.

"I have connections too." Derek stretched out on his side. "My father's the deputy mayor."

"The governor of Vermont offered me fifty-thousand dollars for my virginity. So there." She stuck her tongue out at him.

"Are you serious?"

"No." Xenia laid down a book of cards. "It was Connecticut."

Groaning, Derek rolled onto his back. "If 50K and a governorship doesn't do it for you, then I have no chance, right?" he asked, still smiling.

"The governor of Connecticut never played Go Fish with me. And he's ugly. You aren't. Alanna said you look like Paul Walker. I have no idea who that is, but apparently it's a compliment."

"Well, you look like…" Derek tried to find

someone beautiful enough to compare Xenia to but came up short. "You look like you."

Blushing, she looked down and rearranged her cards in girlish nervousness. Part of him wanted to kiss her again and kiss her for a good three hours. But although he sat on her bed, he didn't quite feel comfortable making a move on her. The virginity thing he considered only a small stumbling block. Xenia's three roommates constituted a slightly larger problem. Derek had wondered how Kingsley could be so sure his mermaids behaved themselves. And Urs said they lived in gorgeous apartments the club paid for—and, yes, Xenia's apartment, located in the building next to the club, qualified as gorgeous. Expansive and elegant, with hardwood floors, lofted ceilings, and—

"Derek, seriously, we don't care how awesome the apartment was," Christian interrupted.

"Sorry, sorry." Derek held up his hands in surrender. "Mom's a real-estate agent. Crown molding is in my genes. Anyway, the apartment was amazing but annoying because Xenia had three roommates. And all four beds were scattered around the big main room."

"That's insidious. I guess that's one way of

keeping your mermaids virginal—put them in dorms with chaperones." Mark shook his head. "This Kingsley Edge guy is an evil genius."

"Oh, God, Kingsley. We'll get back to him in a minute," Derek said.

Xenia beat Derek at their first and second game of Go Fish. As they played they talked about everything and nothing. Derek learned Xenia grew up right on the ocean.

"Probably why I'm still a virgin," she told him as she shuffled her card deck. "My parents run a bed-and-breakfast on Hilton Head Island. Everyone I met was a temporary resident. They'd stay a week maybe, or a month at the most and then be gone again. You learned to guard your heart, not get too attached. The only thing that ever seemed permanent to me was the ocean."

She'd opened her heart a little to him so he told her about his brief marriage that had ended in disaster and had temporarily shattered his faith in women. He even told her about his two best friends, Mark and Christian, who'd helped him through that nightmare three years ago.

"Aww...I'm touched, man," Mark said, pretending to wipe a tear from his eye.

"Shut up," Christian ordered. "I have a feeling things are about to get torrid again."

"You are correct, sir," Derek said.

AROUND THREE IN THE MORNING, he and Xenia gave up on the cards and simply lay on her bed talking while Derek played with her hair. After fifteen minutes, he decided he didn't care if one of her roommates—a Nubian goddess named Alara—sat reading in her bed across the room. He leaned over Xenia, kissing her long and slow. With a sigh of pleasure, she wrapped her arms around his shoulders and pulled him closer. He felt like a teenager again making out with a beautiful girl without any expectations of getting laid. He wanted to touch her, to slip his hands under her shirt and caress her breasts. He wanted to slide his fingers into her little shorts and find out if she was as wet as he was hard. But he merely held her and kissed her and decided if it never progressed farther than this kiss, he would be okay with that.

At about 3:30, a knock on the door interrupted them. A girl so beautiful she had to be another mermaid entered without waiting for a response and looked at Alara and Xenia.

"Coming, Ladies?" the girl asked. She didn't seem the least troubled by Derek's presence in the room.

"I don't know." Xenia rolled up and rearranged her hair. "I hate goodbyes."

"I know," the intruder agreed. "But Emelia wants us there."

Nodding, Xenia stood up.

"Where—" Derek began but Xenia covered his mouth with a quick kiss.

"Don't tell," she whispered and took his hand.

Derek, Xenia, and her roommate followed the girl down a hallway to another room. In the room, Derek saw nothing but a bed covered in white satin sheets ringed with candles. Xenia, Derek, and her roommate stayed in the shadows at the edge of the room and sat on floor pillows. Derek put his arm around Xenia and let her back rest against his chest.

"Are you okay?" he whispered to her when he noticed a tear rolling down her face.

"It's just really sad when one of us leaves. Emelia's like a sister. I wanted to pretend she wasn't really going. Now I can't anymore."

"So is this some sort of going away party?"

Derek asked, seeing the dozen or more mermaids that lined the room.

Xenia shook her head and pressed closer to him. "It's not a party."

After a minute or two, Emelia entered the room wearing a beautiful white silk nightgown. It displayed her ample cleavage but trailed all the way to the floor. Her black hair curled magnificently down her back. She wore no jewelry other than her mermaid pendant around her neck. Gazing at her glowing face, he thought she looked like a virgin bride on her wedding night.

If she was the bride, he had to wonder who her groom could possibly be. But just as he had the thought, Kingsley Edge entered the room and shut the door behind him. He strode to where Emelia stood waiting by the bed, twisting her fingers nervously. Bending his mouth to her ear, he whispered something to the scared girl as he raised his hand and lightly stroked the side of her face.

"Xenia," Derek whispered. "They're not—"

But Xenia didn't answer. She only turned her face up to him, kissed him, and looked back at Kingsley and Emelia.

Whatever Kingsley whispered to Emelia, it seemed to help. She nodded her head and

Kingsley took her face in both hands. Gently, he kissed her. Then the kiss grew deeper, more passionate. Kingsley ran his hands up and down Emelia's back and lingered on her hips. Derek's chest tightened when he realized what was happening right in front of him.

Kingsley's mouth moved from Emelia's lips to the top of her breasts. Slowly he slipped her nightgown off her shoulders and let it cascade like white water to the floor. Sitting on the side of the bed, he pulled Emelia to him and took a nipple in his mouth while his hands continued to caress her stomach and thighs. He pulled back and said something softly to Emelia, gave her some kind of order. Obediently, she lay on the bed and opened her legs.

Quickly and using white silk scarves, Kingsley bound Emelia's hands and wrists to the bedposts, tying her down spread-eagle. Once he had her securely tied, Kingsley straddled her hips and kissed her breasts again. His mouth slid from her nipples to her stomach and then came down between her thighs.

Derek was torn between the red-blooded male in him that wanted to watch and his conscience, which whispered he shouldn't be witness to such a private moment. He glanced down at Xenia and saw her following the scene intently. Her eyes held no hunger, only sadness coupled with interest. Clearly, she grieved for the girl who would leave their little coven but still, she seemed fascinated to witness an act she had never participated in.

Emelia's breasts rose and fell as she panted with pleasure. She gripped the scarves in her fingers, her hips raised off the bed, and she came with a loud, throaty gasp.

As Emelia lay on her back and breathed, Kingsley rose up and pushed a single finger into her. A second finger followed and Derek saw Emelia twitch with either pleasure or pain. Kingsley's fingers moved in and out of her slowly and then side to side. Kingsley spread his fingers apart inside the girl and the sound that escaped Emelia's lips clearly indicated pain. But Kingsley worked patiently on her, and after a few minutes he pushed a third finger into her and made spirals inside her with his hand.

Slowly, meticulously he opened her more and more, his fingers digging deeper and deeper into her. He massaged her clitoris with his other hand. Once again her wrists pulled against her bonds, once again her back arched as another orgasm gripped her.

Kingsley pulled his fingers out of Emelia.

He unbuttoned his shirt and tossed it aside. Derek wanted to look away as Kingsley opened his pants, rolled on a condom, and positioned himself between Emelia's wide-open thighs. But instead of feeling like he was watching some sort of creepy sex show, Derek felt like he was witness to something beautiful and brave. Very brave. Extremely well-endowed, Kingsley, although rich, handsome, and French, might not have been Emelia's best choice for her first lover.

Derek watched as Emelia took a steadying breath and focused her eyes on the ceiling. Kingsley bent his head to her ear. Once more he whispered something to her. Once more she whispered back. Emelia's eyes met Kingsley's. She nodded her head and took a quick hard breath. At the end of her exhale, Kingsley obliterated the girl's virginity with one fierce thrust.

Xenia flinched in Derek's arms, and he held her even tighter. For a long time, Kingsley didn't move. He simply let Emelia breathe and cry. Arching in pain, she pulled on her silken bonds while Kingsley continued to whisper reassurances to her. After a few minutes, her agonized breathing settled. Carefully Kingsley began to move inside her. The whimpering continued but when Kingsley reached between their bodies and found her clitoris, the sound ceased to be agonizing and instead turned rapturous.

Xenia shifted in Derek's arms and he swallowed a groan as her small shapely bottom pressed against his erection. He couldn't help but imagine Xenia underneath him like that, his body inside hers. What an honor it would be to be her first lover, to be the one she gave up Fathoms for. But he remembered Urs, the bitterness and regret in her voice. She'd left Fathoms for someone like him, and now she couldn't come back except as an outsider. Would Xenia regret leaving the way Urs did?

After what seemed like an eternity of slow tortured thrusts, Kingsley began to move faster inside Emelia. The wave of pain had seemingly passed, and now sounds of bliss alone escaped her lips.

Derek tensed as Kingsley increased his pace and moved harder against Emelia. Kingsley gathered her to him as she buried her head against his chest. A shudder wracked Emelia's body as she climaxed a third time. Kingsley thrust once more and came with a sharp intake of breath.

Slowly, Kingsley pulled out of her and

Derek saw the blood on him. He closed his pants, pulled on his shirt, and untied Emelia. Rolling up, Emelia slipped back into her gown, wincing a little with every small movement. Finally, she reached up and unclasped the mermaid pendant from around her neck. She reached for Kingsley's hand and placed it in the center of his palm. He wrapped his fingers around it like a cherished gift and kissed the back of her hand.

Emelia turned away from him and left the room, a hint of tears at the corner of her eyes.

"Oh...my...God...." Christian said, and Derek nearly laughed at the expressions on Mark and Christian's faces. They looked like the proverbial deer in headlights.

"I know," Derek agreed. "That's how I felt."

"I can't believe you got to watch Kingsley Edge tie some girl down and take her virginity right in front of you," Mark breathed. "You lucky fucking son of a bitch."

"I didn't feel lucky right then. Privileged, sort of. But also freaked out. Not kidding, the bloodstain on the bed was as big as your hand. And I was there. Kingsley was incredibly careful and that girl was still in agony half the time. I'd say it was as sobering as it was sexy."

"My first time was with a virgin," Mark said. "She was fifteen, I was sixteen. After that first time she wouldn't let me near her for three months, that's how much it hurt."

"Or she just didn't like you anymore, and she used that as an excuse," Christian posited.

"Highly probable," Mark agreed. "But continue, you pervert. I've got to hear what happened next."

"What happened next," Derek began, "was me spending a couple of minutes on the floor trying to will my erection away. No amount of imagining dead relatives or my parents having sex seemed to work. So Xenia sat down in front of me and started telling me about Emelia. About how she came from this poor family of about eight kids, and how she couldn't even afford community college until Kingsley found her working at some Catholic charity when she was nineteen."

"Catholic charity?"

"Supposedly Kingsley's brother-in-law is a priest. Don't ask—I didn't. Anyway, talking about Emelia as a person who wanted to do nothing except help people helped me get to the point I could stand up again without coming all over myself."

"Then what did you two do?" Christian asked, his eyes gleaming with mirth.

"I did something absolutely insane at that moment. I asked Xenia to spend the next day with me. And she said 'yes.'"

Derek left shortly after that. Both he and Xenia had to get some sleep. But he promised her he'd pick her up in front of Cirque du Nuit later that day. Once he returned to his apartment, he took a fifteen-minute shower. Only five minutes of the shower involved actual showering. The other ten minutes involved him relieving the pressure of the four most sexually frustrating hours of his life.

❧

HE SLEPT like the dead until noon, got up, showered, relieved the lingering pressure again, and dressed for a day out. At one o'clock, he pulled up in front of Cirque du Nuit right as Xenia emerged from the entryway wearing a sleeveless white cotton dress and very dark sunglasses.

"Trying not to be recognized?" he asked as he opened the door of his Audi for her.

"I haven't been out in the sun for a while," she admitted. "I'd forgotten how bright the day is. If you can talk someone into turning down the sun a little, I'll take them off."

"You look beautiful. I just miss your eyes. We can hang out in the shade if you want."

She shook her head. "Let's go to the park and walk. I haven't done that in forever."

They hit Central Park a little after one and strolled the winding walkways, dodging dogs and joggers the entire time.

"So last night," Derek began.

"You think we're crazy, right?"

"A little. But not bad crazy. Is that...typical?"

Xenia laughed and took a bite of the pretzel he'd bought for her. "Kingsley's done the honors for us more than once. A lot of us would have nothing without him. And we all live together, swim around naked together.... Emelia wanted to share that really important moment in her life with us."

"You weren't planning on something like that, were you?" Derek asked.

"I do love Kingsley. But like a brother only. Promise." She smiled at the relief that shone on his face. "Obviously there are worse guys to have your first time with than Kingsley. The guy Urs left us for was a total ass. He paid her for her virginity, so much she couldn't say 'no,' and then after some extremely bad, painful sex, decides that being with a virgin's over-rated. He dumped her after a week. At least she got the money first."

Having a virginal girlfriend had its drawbacks. But the thought of instructing Xenia in the bedroom, learning along with her how her body worked, turned him on so much he was in danger of needing yet another therapeutic shower.

"What an asshole. I know guys who would kill for a girl as gorgeous as her without all the ex-boyfriend baggage," Derek said, unable to even dream of doing that to Xenia.

"Me, for one," Mark chimed in. "Do you have this Urs person's phone number? She's feisty and wasn't afraid to chew you out. I like her already."

"No, sorry. But trust me, the girl's got some serious anger issues. You'll see."

They talked as they walked, and once Xenia finished her pretzel, she twined her fingers into Derek's and, hand-in-hand, they strolled the park.

"Are your feet getting tired?" he asked her as her pace started to slacken.

"A little. I do all my working out in the water. I weigh a lot less in liquid."

"Here. Let's get some wheels."

The wheels in question also included a horse. Derek had always thought the carriage ride through Central Park seemed too cliché to be even remotely enjoyable. But Xenia's face lit up around the horse and suddenly the cliché did actually seem almost romantic.

"This is fantastic," Xenia said. "I can't remember the last time I stayed out all day in the sun."

"The club takes over your life, does it?"

She nodded. "You meet the most interesting people. But it sort of screws up your schedule. I'm up all night and sleep all day."

"Are you a vampire or a mermaid?"

"Both." She playfully bit his neck.

The play bite turned into a kiss, and the kiss turned into another long make-out session in the carriage.

"The making out has to stop, Derek. It just does. At least get to second base with the damn girl," Mark ordered.

"Fine, fine. The day went great. Best date of my life. Talked, laughed…. She was smart and funny and had a ton of stories to tell me about famous weirdos she met."

"Don't care. Skip to the good parts."

"Every second with Xenia was a good

part," Derek said, feeling the truth of the statement in his heart. Every moment he spent with her he felt awake, alive. Not just like Derek Prince, but Derek Princely.

"Yo, Prince Derek. Get back to the story."

"Fine, fine."

Hours later, Derek dropped Xenia off at the club. The kiss in the carriage couldn't compete with the passionate kiss he received as they said goodbye. As soon as they parted, he began counting the hours until he could see her again. Her shift ended at two on Saturdays, so he had a few hours to kill. He killed them by working and sleeping. Her vampire hours seemed a bigger annoyance than her virginity had been so far. But still, he wondered how long he could go without consummating his intense passion for her.

Two a.m. found Derek in the lounge waiting once more for Xenia. Once more she appeared in the doorway naked and dripping wet. This time he could meet her eyes without staring at her breasts first.

"Hey you," she said, grinning from ear to ear. "I've got to get my rubdown on, but I'll be done in just a few minutes, okay?"

"Not okay. I know the massage skincare thing is part of the routine, but I will go insane if I have to sit in here while some guy paws at you in the next room."

Laughing, she rolled her eyes. "Not all of us take advantage of that particular perk of the job. For the record, I never have. It's just skin and hair care, very much needed in this line of work."

"That and getting a pretty personal inspection."

She shrugged. "Part of the job. You saw where we live, how well we're treated. All Kingsley asks is that we stay virgins while we work here. Small price to pay from where I stand."

"There's gotta be a compromise. I'm having a hard enough time thinking about all those men downstairs drooling all over you."

"I'm constantly wet," she teased. "A little drool is not a big deal. But we can compromise on this if you want."

He eyed her warily. Her tone was a bit too mischievous to be entirely trustworthy. "What's the compromise?"

"You can give me my rubdown. How's that?"

They crossed the hallway to the massage studio. With great relief, Derek discovered that the door locked. Just being near Xenia's body put him in a state of extreme arousal. He preferred as few witnesses as possible to his uncontrollable erection.

He took off his jacket and rolled up the sleeves of his white button-down as Xenia positioned herself on her stomach. Derek couldn't look at her like that without imagining himself on top of her, his chest to her back, his hands in her hair, thrusting into her from behind.

Taking a low slow breath, Derek reminded himself that he was doing this for Xenia and not as some sort of sexual act. He convinced his mind. His body remained dubious.

"What first?" he asked.

"Hair. That's the blue bottle. I can do that myself if you want."

"No. I'm going to do this right," Derek said and took the blue glass bottle off the table and poured vanilla-scented oil into his palms. He started at the nape of Xenia's neck and massaged it all the way through her long wavy hair. She sighed contentedly while Derek played with her hair.

"I think I got every strand, probably twice," he said. "What now?"

"Gold stuff. That's for the body. Watch my

feet though. I'm ticklish and if you rub too lightly, I'll kick you."

"Good to know." Derek washed the hair serum off his hands and poured a mound of the pale golden oil into his palms. He started at Xenia's shoulders and rubbed his way down her back.

"God, this stuff smells amazing," Derek said as the scent wafted up to his nose. "It smells like the ocean and orchids."

"This place in uptown makes it just for us. No one but Kingsley's mermaids gets to use it. The silver metallic ink is ours alone too. This brilliant tattoo artist in the Village invented the stuff. No other tattoo artist in the world has this kind of ink."

"Did they hurt?" Derek asked, tracing the tattoos of fish scales on her hips.

"A little. But it's a badge of honor to have them. You can't wear the mermaid pendant anymore once you lose your virginity, but you have the tattoos for life."

Derek moved from her back to her bottom, and Xenia giggled a little as he lingered unnecessarily over his work.

"I have legs too, you know," she reminded him.

"Legs. Right." Derek worked his way

down the back of her legs, massaging oil into her thighs, her calves, and the bottom of her feet. "I think I'm done with your exquisite backside. Unfortunately."

"No worries. One side left."

She flipped over onto her back and gazed at him through half-closed eyes. Derek cursed himself for not taking yet another therapeutic shower right before coming to Fathoms.

He started at her arms because they seemed safe to touch. But he could only linger there for so long. He poured a line of oil down the center of Xenia's body from her collarbone to her bellybutton. Laying his hands on her chest, he rubbed her neck and shoulders before sliding down to her breasts. He nearly moaned aloud as he finally touched her beautiful perfect breasts. No amount of reminding himself his job was to massage and not to grope could keep him from cupping them in his hands and caressing her nipples until they grew stiff and rosy.

"I usually fall asleep during this," she said, a desperate catch in her voice.

"Not feeling sleepy?" he asked as he gently teased her nipples between his thumb and forefinger.

She shook her head. "I'm feeling everything *but* sleepy."

"Good," he breathed as he moved reluctantly from her breasts to her stomach. From her stomach, he moved to her hips and massaged the tops of her legs down to her feet and back again. On his way back up her body, she spread her knees wide enough for him to slip his hands between them. As he neared the apex of her thighs, he could feel heat radiating from her.

"You can touch me, Derek," she whispered. "I want you to."

His hands almost shaking from raw need, Derek caressed the smooth outer folds until Xenia pulled her legs even wider apart. He slid his finger down the wet slit and pressed the lips of her vagina wide open.

"Xenia…you're so…God." He couldn't find the words. "Are you sure this is allowed?"

"Just be careful," she said, and Derek knew what she meant. Right in front of his eyes, he could see the thin membrane of tissue that stretched across the lower half of the entrance to her body.

Wary of her hymen, Derek slowly slid one finger inside Xenia. Heat and wetness enveloped his finger as he pushed in as far as he could go. Xenia's breath caught in her throat; her breasts rose and fell.

"That's incredible," she said, exhaling heavily.

"God, it is," he agreed, moving inside her tight wet passage, pressing into her g-spot, finding all the places that sent her panting. Pushing lightly into the front wall, Derek saw Xenia twitch and then grin. With his other hand, Derek massaged her clitoris, which swelled at his touch. Derek rubbed harder and quicker, letting his pace match the rhythm of Xenia's ragged breathing. He ached to open his pants, climb on the table, and thrust into her for the rest of his life. But he held back and only touched her with his hands.

Her back arched and every muscle in her body seemed to tense at once. With a quiet, hard gasp, Xenia climaxed. Derek nearly came from the sensation of her inner muscles as they spasmed around his finger. Carefully he pulled out of her as Xenia rolled up. She wrapped her arms around him and brought her mouth to his.

"Xenia, we should stop," Derek said, wanting to do anything but. "I'm seriously about to lose whatever self-control I had two minutes ago."

"Let me help," she said into his lips. "Let me touch you too."

She reached down and unzipped his jeans. Derek rested his forehead on her shoulder as she took his desperately hard length in her hands. Lightly she touched him, her fingers skimming his skin so gently he almost screamed. When she wrapped both small hands around him, Derek couldn't hold back any longer. He came with a fierce gasp, shuddering harder than he ever had in his life.

"I'll get a towel," he said, embarrassed that he'd come so hard and so quickly right on her hands.

Xenia looked at her hand before raising her palm to her lips. She touched his semen lightly with the tip of her tongue.

"Tastes like the ocean," she concluded.

The sight of her tasting him out of nothing but innocent curiosity brought his blood quickly back to a boil. His mouth crashed onto hers as he pushed her onto her back. Instead of touching her nipples, he sucked them hard while his finger pushed inside her again. He pulled her hips to the end of the table and shoved her legs over his shoulders. Dipping his head, he took her clitoris between his lips and stroked it with his tongue. He devoured her with his mouth until she came once more, this time even harder than the first.

As she caught her breath, Derek kissed his way back up her body to her mouth. "You taste better than the ocean," he said as he let her taste herself on his lips.

She opened her mouth to say something, but a knock on the door interrupted their erotic reverie.

"Shit," Derek said, handing Xenia a towel.

"It's okay. I've got it."

Xenia wrapped the towel around herself and opened the door. Urs waited outside the door.

"Sorry, Urs. Did you need the room?" Xenia asked, nothing but sweet solicitude in her voice.

"No. But you two need to get a room. And you need to give up the pendant, Xenia." Urs held out her hand.

Xenia shook her head. "We didn't have sex. We were just—"

"Just what? I'm not deaf."

Derek stepped forward and between the two women. "Urs, it's my fault. We got carried away. But no, we didn't have sex."

"Really? Prove it," Urs said and pointed at the table.

"No. I don't want to—" Xenia began.

"Then give up the pendant."

"I will not," Xenia said and took a step back.

"Give it up," Urs demanded, reaching for Xenia's throat. With more force than he ever dreamed he'd use on a woman, Derek grabbed Urs's arm before her fingers could touch Xenia.

"Urs," Derek said quietly, coldly, "back off."

"I don't answer to you, Urs," Xenia said, standing up to her full and utterly unimpressive height.

"*Non*, but you do answer to *moi*," said a voice from the end of the hallway. Derek released Urs's arm as Kingsley strolled toward them. "Now what is this about?"

"Xenia and Derek were having sex in the massage room. She won't give up her pendant."

Kingsley looked at Derek and Xenia then back at Urs. "Is this true, Xenia?" he asked them.

She shook her head. "We didn't have sex."

"She says that," Urs said, "but she won't prove it."

"I can prove it," Xenia said. Derek saw

frustrated tears in her eyes. "I don't care. It's fine."

"No, it isn't fine. Urs doesn't get to put you in stirrups just because she heard us fooling around."

"Then I will," Kingsley said calmly. "Xenia, after you."

Xenia bit her bottom lip and started to step back into the room. Before Kingsley could follow, Derek thrust his arm out and barred Kingsley's way. He heard both Xenia and Urs gasp aloud.

"Derek, don't," Xenia warned. But Derek paid no heed. Rarely if ever had he felt he could kill someone. But now an animal rage welled up in him, a fierce protectiveness that surged through his blood and shocked even him with its ferocity.

"Mr. Edge," Derek said, his voice so bitterly angry even he barely recognized it. "I know you've called all sorts of politicians in your book. I know people who call you the most dangerous man in the city. But if you touch her in any way she doesn't want..." Derek took a long slow breath. "I don't know when, and I don't know how, but I will make you regret it."

"Jesus, Derek, you really said that to Kingsley Edge?" Christian asked.

"That was it almost word for word," Derek confessed, recalling that moment in crystal clear detail. He remembered it so well because at the time he thought it might be the last few minutes of his life.

"Dude, Kingsley's ex-French Foreign Legion. You're lucky to be alive. What did he do?"

"He smiled."

The smile scared him more than wrath would have. Kingsley smiled like a man unafraid of anything or anyone—especially him.

"I like you, *Monsieur* Prince. But rules are rules. Xenia?"

Her bottom lip quivering, Xenia stepped back into the room. Kingsley ducked under Derek's arm, and closed the door behind him.

The minute Derek waited in the hall safely qualified as the longest minute of his life.

"You psychotic bitch," Derek said, his eyes narrowing at Urs.

"Your own fault. You know the rules here. She gets to stay as long as she's a virgin. Once she isn't, she's gone. You having sex with her doesn't just affect you, it affects her whole life. Do you get that?"

Before he could answer, Xenia emerged from the room and slipped into Derek's arms. Kingsley followed and gave Derek another smile before strolling off.

"Urs," Kingsley called back, "back to work."

Urs brushed past them and headed back downstairs.

"Are you okay?" Derek whispered into her hair.

"He didn't touch me. He didn't do anything but ask me to look him in the eyes and tell him the truth."

"So he didn't…?"

"No. He didn't."

Derek heaved a sigh of relief and prayed Xenia wasn't lying just to keep him from killing her boss. "If he made you spread your legs for him, would you have?" he asked, afraid of the answer.

Xenia looked at the ceiling. "He's seen it before."

"So that's a 'yes'?"

"It's the price you pay for working here."

"It's worth it?" he asked.

Slowly, Xenia nodded. "It's my home."

A cold, miserable realization settled into Derek's mind and sunk into his stomach.

"You really love this place. And I can't ask you to leave it. But if I stick around, something's going to happen and they'll make you."

"Derek, I don't want to leave. But I don't want to lose you either. I've never felt anything like what I feel with you."

"And I've never, God, I was married, Xenia, and I never felt anything like this. I threatened to kill Kingsley Edge. I must have a death wish."

"It was impressive. I think he likes you even more now. I do too."

Derek rubbed his face. "I can't do this. I can't put you in the position to choose between this place you love and some guy you barely know."

"Don't be like this. We can figure something out. We can—"

"What? What can we do?"

"I don't know." Her voice was no more than a whisper.

Derek squeezed his eyes shut tight. He pulled out his wallet and dug out his business card. "Here. It's got all my numbers on it. When you decide to leave here, call me. I'll come running. But I won't put you in this position again. I'm sorry," he said.

Xenia looked down at the card in his hand but didn't take it.

"Do you know how men have tried to give me their business cards?" she asked, her eyes going cold, her voice hollow. "More than I can begin to count. Do you know what I did when they offered me their business cards?"

Derek swallowed hard. "No."

"I did this." Xenia dropped her towel, walked to the edge of the column, and dove into the water. Dove in and dove deep and showed no sign of coming back up for a long time.

⚜

"AND THAT," Derek said, finishing his drink off, "is the end of my story."

"Whoa, there. No way," Mark said. "She never gave you her mermaid?"

"No, she didn't." Derek stood up and tossed a hundred on the table. "And now it's almost midnight and I'm about to turn into a pumpkin."

"Get your ass back here and finish the story, Derek."

"I already told you, that's the end. See you at work on Monday."

Smiling to himself, Derek left Mark and Christian cursing him. On the way to his apartment, he remembered how he felt that moment Xenia slipped away from him, when she dove into the pool and turned into nothing but foam on the surface of the water. He couldn't believe she wouldn't even take his card...but then he realized what giving her his business card meant—it meant he wouldn't see her anymore unless she'd have sex with him. And the ache in his heart at the thought of never seeing her again trumped the ache in his body at the chance they'd never make love.

So he'd done the only thing a man could do when in love with a mermaid who was swimming away from him. He dove in after her. Even underwater, he saw her eyes go comically wide. She raced to the surface, where Derek was treading water, clinging to the side of the pool.

"I'm sorry," he said. "I'm an idiot. I can't ask you to leave your life here, but I don't want to lose you. So let's stay together and see if we can work."

"Derek, I can't be with you the way you want me to be and stay here."

"Doesn't matter," he said, meaning every word. "When you're ready, we'll go for it.

Until then, I'll just take a lot of cold showers. Starting right now. This water is fucking freezing."

"Keeps the nipples hard," she said, grinning. "You really mean it?"

"Take all the time you need. I just want to be part of your world. I need you in my life any way that works for you."

"And I need you in my life."

"And I need you out of my pool," said a voice from above them. Derek looked up and saw Kingsley glaring down at him from the edge of the water. *"S'il vous plait."*

After they'd dried off, Xenia, Derek, and Kingsley had a long talk. Xenia could continue to work at Fathoms and see Derek as long as they didn't have intercourse. Technical virginity was good enough for Kingsley. "I am French after all," he reminded them.

And Kingsley agreed to allow one of the other mermaids to handle Xenia's rubdowns and virginity checks, which Derek already looked forward to watching.

"You're a fool, *Monsieur*," Kingsley warned Derek. "So many beautiful girls in the city who would willingly dive into your bed. And you give that up."

"I don't want a girl. I want a mermaid."

Derek arrived at his apartment still smiling at the story he'd told Mark and Christian. As he put the key into his lock, Derek spied a small puddle of water outside his door.

Opening the door, he found Xenia inside wearing the white skirt and cami he'd first seen her in.

She ran to him and threw her arms around him. "Happy anniversary."

"One year," he said, kissing her deep and slow. "Seems like yesterday."

"It's not the only anniversary we have to celebrate today."

"Really? What's the other one?" he asked, gently playing with the mermaid pendant that still hung around her neck.

"Today is the two-week anniversary of me putting in my two-weeks notice at Fathoms."

Derek only stared at her. "You're kidding."

She shook her head. "No. I'm ready. Not just for you but for everything. Life. School maybe. The real world. And I'm ready for this."

Slipping her hands behind her neck, she unclasped her mermaid pendant and laid it in the palm of Derek's hand.

"I can't accept this gift," he said solemnly.

Xenia's eyes fell. "Why not?"

"It's too precious for you to just give it away."

"But—"

"How about a trade?"

Derek reached into his pocket and pulled out a large, shimmering sapphire and diamond ring—sapphire, the color of the ocean, the color of Xenia's eyes.

Kneeling down on one knee, Derek opened his mouth but Xenia gave him no chance to speak. She threw her arms around him and sobbed into his shoulder.

"This is a 'yes,' right?" he asked, trembling.

She nodded, but no words came out.

"We can wait as long as you want," he said. "For the wedding. For sex. Whatever you want."

"I want you," she whispered as he slipped the ring on her left hand. "Tonight."

Derek took her in his arms and carried her into his bedroom. He hadn't even let himself hope this would happen tonight. The past year had been a lesson in endurance for him. Some nights, he wouldn't even let her come over because the need in him burned too hotly. But after a few months, she ceased to be an object of sexual obsession and became instead his closest friend. With sex off the table, they had to improvise. They talked for hours, went for walks, went dancing. Derek finally learned how to beat her in Go Fish—he cheated just like she did. He learned she loved the Go-Go's and white chocolate and could speak French and Persian fluently. She started to go out more. Six months ago, she had started giving swimming lessons at a local gym. Last month, he met her parents. Last week, she met his. And next week she'd finally get to meet Mark and Christian.

They hadn't been saints during the past year, of course. Not even his ex-wife or Ireland knew his body as well as Xenia did now. Her nimble fingers and full lips and tongue could send him to the heights of erotic ecstasy. And with his mouth and one finger, he could make her wake the neighbors. Tonight he wanted to make her wake the whole town.

Derek laid her back on the bed and slowly undressed her. Even after a year with his little exhibitionist mermaid, he never ceased to be moved by the sight of her naked curves. He kissed her lips, her neck and chest. She dug her hands into his hair as he took a nipple into his mouth as his hand sought her other breast.

He wanted their first time together to be as painless as possible. He wanted her wet inside and aching for him.

"Derek, please," she begged.

"Patience," he teased. "You made me wait a year. It's only fair I make you wait a few more minutes."

Still dressed, Derek spread her legs and sat between her open thighs. He opened her folds and slipped a finger into her. As usual, she sighed blissfully and lifted her hips to take him in deeper. For the first time ever, Derek turned his hand and pressed a second finger inside her. He felt the barrier of her virginity against his fingers.

"Tell me if it hurts," he said softly.

"Feels wonderful."

He took her clitoris between his thumb and index finger and gently massaged it. Xenia's head fell back in pleasure while Derek pushed down on her hymen. He put both thumbs in her, gripped her hips, and pulled her wider open. Bending over her, he took a nipple in his mouth again and sucked deeply while he slowly pushed a third finger into her. He wanted her on the edge of orgasm when he penetrated her the first time.

"Derek...." she groaned.

Derek pressed his forehead to hers. "Xenia, I don't want to hurt you."

Xenia laid her hand on the side of his face. His fingers still rested deep inside her.

"*Your tail will then disappear*," Xenia quoted softly, meeting Derek's eyes. "*And shrink up into what mankind calls legs, and you will feel great pain, as if a sword were passing through you.*"

"What is that?" he asked.

"It's from *The Little Mermaid*, the fairy tale. It's what a mermaid feels when she becomes a human woman. Great pain. Derek, I'm ready to be human."

A tiny knot formed in Derek's throat. In Xenia's eyes he saw not a single flicker of fear —only love, trust, and desire.

He kissed her once, pulled away from her, and undressed. Naked now he stretched on top of her. Xenia opened her legs for him and he pressed the tip of his straining erection against her hymen.

"I love you," he whispered and thrust fast and hard into the very core of her. He gasped, his eyes wide open. It had been over a year since he'd been inside a woman's body. His heart pounded in his chest, blood throbbed in his ears. Staying in her without moving, without pumping madly into her, strained every ounce of Derek's self-control.

An anguished whimper from underneath him brought Derek back to himself.

"Breathe," he begged Xenia, running his hand through her hair. "Try to breathe."

Xenia nodded and buried her head against his chest. All around him he felt her heat, her wetness, and her tight inner muscles trying to push him out of her. Wrapping his arms around her, he rolled them onto their sides. He rubbed her lower back and hips, massaging them until her muscles started to unknot.

"Do you want to stop?" he asked, kissing the tear on her cheek.

"Never." She smiled at him and tentatively pressed her hips into his.

Groaning, Derek pushed her onto her back again and thrust deep. He breathed slowly, willing himself to hold back. But Xenia's body held him like a hand. Her clitoris swelled at his touch. With short sharp thrusts he moved in her, trying to mask her pain with pleasure.

Taking her legs in his hands, he pushed them as wide as they could go. He moved more easily inside her now. With long full thrusts he rode her, relishing the sensation of her body wrapped around his.

Finally, he heard Xenia's breathing change. He'd learned long ago that when her breaths turned sharp and shallow, she was close to coming. Locking his arms over either side of her shoulders, he increased his pace, moving in her with thrusts both meticulous and frenzied.

Pressure built deep in his hips. Xenia cried out under him as her climax sent her body clenching wildly around his. With a last thrust, Derek clutched her to him, pushed once more, and poured into her.

Afterward, Derek lingered inside her, kissing her lips, her face, her forehead.

"Was it worth waiting for?" he asked. He knew his answer—yes. And he would have gladly waited longer.

Xenia wrapped her arms around his neck and sank into the sheets. Sighing tiredly, she smiled. "It was worth everything."

After a few minutes of simply enjoying being inside her, Derek slid out of her. He washed the blood off them, pleased to see the damage hadn't been as bad as he feared. Xenia surprised him by wanting to try again almost immediately. With the aid of some lubricant and an hour of foreplay, they managed to make love again, this time without pain. Derek stood at the side of the bed and moved in Xenia as she lay on her back, her hips at the edge of the mattress. Next he would teach her doggy style, then woman superior…maybe they'd just start the beginning of the Kama Sutra and work their way through it. He felt like a virgin himself in a way—until tonight, until Xenia, he'd never made love.

Finally spent they lay on their sides, Xenia's back nestled against his chest.

"You think Kingsley will come to the wedding?" Derek asked, kissing the silver fin tattoo on her shoulder.

"No. But knowing him, he'll try to come on the honeymoon."

Derek laughed as he lightly teased her nipples with his fingertips. "Honeymoon sounds good. The ocean?"

"Of course," she said, pressing her bottom into his growing erection. Maybe they'd try it from behind this time. "No kids though. Nothing bigger than you is ever going in or coming out of me."

"I won't argue with that. Dogs then?"

"Dogs need yards. Cats?" Xenia suggested.

"I'm allergic. So no kids, no dogs, no cats. Hmmm…Wait, I've got it."

Xenia turned over and grinned at him through the dark. Even in the low light, he could see the childlike mischief in her eyes. Ten years from now, a hundred years from now, he would still love those ocean eyes.

"What?" she asked.

He ran his fingertips over her face and down her arms, and then traced the tattoos that adorned her hips.

"Fish."

SUBMIT TO DESIRE

SUBMIT
TO
DESIRE

"Another one bites the dust," Charlotte said, raising her glass. Two other glasses met it, and the resulting clink sent Amaretto Sour dripping over her fingers and onto the floor.

"Good riddance to bad boyfriends." London downed the last of her Fuzzy Navel and sat the empty glass on the bar.

"I'll drink to that," Sasha said, sucking out the last drops of her Long Island Iced Tea.

Steele, the bartender, refilled Sasha's glass without a word.

"That's the problem." Charlotte tucked a stray strand of red hair back into her straw cowboy hat. "Nick wasn't a bad boyfriend. He was…nice."

London stared at her over the top of her drink. "You already dumped him, Char," she said. "Don't add insult to injury."

"You women are all the same." Steele set three shots up in front of them. "God forbid you date a guy who's nice to you."

"Nick *was* nice." Sasha picked up her shot. "And kind of hot. Nice isn't bad. Nice is just…boring."

"Boring," London agreed.

Charlotte sighed and gazed down into her drink.

Nick was nice. Too nice. So nice, she wanted to kill him for it sometimes. Last week had been the last straw. She'd fallen asleep during sex. Missionary position. Five minutes of foreplay. Five minutes of thrusting. Ten minutes of "I love everything about you." Just…like…always.

"Boring," Charlotte echoed as she looked up and met the eyes of a man walking through the bar. The man, whoever he was, looked to be in his mid-thirties and had shoulder-length dark hair and olive skin. His suit was almost Victorian-looking, like something off a romance novel cover. And he wasn't walking so much as strolling, as if the crowded nightclub was a park in spring, and he was a country squire out on a pleasant Sunday ramble.

"Steele, who is that guy?" London asked.

Steele gave the three ladies a half-cocked smile. "That is Kingsley Edge. And he is the opposite of boring. And if you three have any sense, you'll stay away from him."

"What sense I had just took her panties off and laid down in front of him," Sasha said with a drunken giggle.

"God, he looks like a pirate." London ran her finger around the rim of her glass.

"I think he looks dangerous." Sasha shot the man her best come-over-here smile.

Charlotte sighed. Sasha and London had promised her a girls' night out to help cheer her up over yet another failed relationship. "No men" had been their promise. Only alcohol and dancing. Maybe it was time to get some better friends.

"He looks like he needs a haircut." Charlotte downed her shot in one bitter swallow.

"Hey, do your trick, Char. That'll get his attention," Sasha begged.

"I don't want to get his attention. He's a pimp." Charlotte had heard of Kingsley Edge. No one who haunted New York's nightlife hadn't. His respectable business interests included owning several of the city's top clubs. Rumors swirled about the man, however…rumors that he made the vast majority of his money pushing flesh and not cocktails.

Steele laughed, and the three friends spun back around on their bar stools. "Kingsley Edge is not a pimp," he said, pouring Charlotte a fresh Amaretto Sour. "Kingsley Edge is a talent scout."

"Talent scout?" Charlotte's eyes followed Kingsley Edge as he made his way through the club. Every few feet, he'd pause and gaze at her through the crowd. "What sort of talent?"

"Maybe your talent." Steele winked at her. She'd worked at this club, Cirque de Nuit, a few years ago and had picked up a trick or two.

Sasha and London looked at Charlotte with pleading eyes. Steele held out a shot glass full of liquid paraffin. Once again, Charlotte decided to make getting new friends a top priority. She was buzzed, but Sasha and London were shitfaced. And they were making her perform for them. Fine—if they insisted.

Charlotte sighed and took the shot glass. Sasha handed her a lighter.

Sasha and London clapped while they hopped off their stools and stood far away. Charlotte noticed that the commotion had not just gotten the attention of most of the nightclub patrons, but had alerted Kingsley Edge as well. He stood next to a column and leaned against it with one eyebrow raised.

Charlotte inhaled deeply, swigged the liquid paraffin, pursed her lips, flicked the lighter and pushed air out so hard her ears popped. A fireball blew out several feet in front of her and set everyone in the nightclub screaming and clapping. She kept blowing even after the fire went out, knowing she had to exhale anything left in her mouth. Hopping off her bar stool, she gave a small bow before turning back to her drink. She'd already had five tonight. One for each nice boyfriend she'd dumped in the last five years.

Two hours later, she lay on the floor in the VIP section. She heard two male voices talking above her. One sounded like Steele's. The other sounded almost melodic…deeply male and as intoxicating as all the alcohol she'd imbibed.

"It's last call, chief. What should I do with her?"

"I'll take care of *le petit dragon*."

"You sure about that?"

She was close to passing out but she remembered the laugh. A warm, low laugh, she felt it more than it heard it. It rolled down her body from her neck to her ankles.

"Quite sure," the voice said in an accent her addled mind recognized as French. "I like a woman with a little fire in her belly."

❧

CHARLOTTE WOKE up in the fetal position. Groaning, she opened her eyes and saw a pair of

knee-high leather riding boots. The boots be-
longed to a pair of long legs crossed at the ankles and using her back as a footstool. Looking
up, she saw Kingsley Edge lounging on the VIP
sofa with a dainty teacup and saucer in his
hands. Sipping at his tea, he smiled down at her.

"I hope you don't mind my saying this,
chérie, but you need a new hobby."

It took her much longer than it should
have to process his words.

"Hobby?" she asked. "Who are you?"

"You know who I am. And I know who
you are." He held up her driver's license and
studied it with his dark eyes. "Charlotte
Brand. Steele tells me your friends call you
Char. Shameful. I'll call you Charlie, if you
don't mind."

"I might mind."

"Twenty-seven," he said, still staring at her
license. "A good age, Charlie."

"You're really going to call me Charlie?"

"*Oui.* I love women with men's names. It
satisfies a certain deviant side to me."

"Is your boot on my back part of your deviant side?" Charlotte sat up, and Kingsley
lifted his feet off her back with a graceful air.

"What can I say? When I see a beautiful

woman so drunk she ends up passed out on the floor, I assume she's there because she wants to be walked all over."

"Nice guilt trip. I heard you were a pimp. Are you a priest, too?"

"*Non.* But I have a priest on speed dial if you need one," he said with a wicked grin on his sculpted lips. "Would you like to come home with me now, Charlie?"

"What are you going to do to me?" His face came into focus for the first time. She'd heard he was French…or half-French, something like that. He was rich and had half the judges and cops in town in his back pocket. She'd also heard he was handsome, but handsome didn't do justice to the man lounging in front of her.

"Breakfast and a shower are in order. Perhaps then we can discuss a certain business opportunity."

The phrase *business opportunity* triggered a memory from last night. Steele said that Kingsley Edge wasn't a pimp but a talent scout. Talent scout—she had a feeling she knew exactly what this *business opportunity* might entail.

"The shower and breakfast might work.

But I can save you the trouble—*no* to any business opportunities."

"You say that now…but wait until you try my pancakes."

He sat his teacup and saucer down and held out his hand. What the hell was she getting herself into?

Charlotte reached out and put her hand into his. Wrapping his fingers around hers, he pulled her to her feet. Wobbling a little on her high heels, she put her hand on his chest to steady herself. He covered her hand with his own and met her eyes.

"You're a beautiful woman." His dark-lashed eyes studied her face. "Even with scuff marks on your cheek."

Charlotte blushed and rubbed her face.

"Don't bother. We'll wash it off at my townhouse. Shall we, Charlie?"

"Okay, so you're going to call me Charlie. What do I call you?"

"Everyone calls me Kingsley or King. Or Monsieur. Take your pick."

"Monsieur?"

"Mon père était français et j'ai servi dans la légion étrangère française."

Charlotte blinked and tried to make out any of the words Kingsley had said. But none of it registered as anything but poetic nonsense.

"I said, 'My father was French and I served in the French Foreign Legion.'"

Charlotte stared at Kingsley. The riding boots...the suit...the arrogance to choose a new nickname for her only moments after meeting her.

"You're a little insane, aren't you, Kingsley?"

He flashed her a wicked grin. "*Oui*, and you are coming home with me."

"Touché."

Kingsley strode off and Charlotte followed him. He paused as he passed the bar and picked up her cowboy hat, which someone had left there. He tossed it to her.

"I'm giving it back to you but don't think you're allowed to wear it in my presence."

"Why not?"

"Because you have the most beautiful claret-colored hair I've ever seen, and it's a crime to cover it."

Charlotte rolled her eyes. "It's not real. Well, the hair's real, but not the color. I'm a hair stylist."

"I don't care if it's real. I wasn't born bilingual, but that doesn't change the fact that it turns you on that I am. *Oui?*"

Kingsley spun on his heel to smile back at her. He raised his eyebrows and seemed to be waiting for her to answer.

"Okay, *oui*," she admitted.

"*J'accepte.*" Kingsley threw open the doors to the club.

Charlotte shielded her face as the morning sunlight beat down on her aching eyes. Once inside the back of Kingsley's car, she noticed the lush leather interior and the old-world feel.

"Holy shit…is this a Rolls-Royce?"

Kingsley sat on the bench seat opposite her. "She is. Not my favorite one, but she's fine for running errands."

"So am I an errand?" Charlotte asked.

"I don't know." Kingsley gave her a long look that set the hairs on her arms standing up. "Are you running?"

Charlotte looked out the window and saw the city regulars on their way to work—men in power suits, women in severe dresses. And here she sat in a Rolls-Royce with one of the city's most notorious underground figures.

"Not yet."

Kingsley grinned. "Good answer, Charlie. Here we are."

The Rolls pulled in front of an elegant black-and-white bricked townhouse three stories high.

Kingsley left the car first and held out his hand for her. She tried to stay steady on her feet as he pulled her out of the car. Inside the townhouse, Kingsley steered her up two flights of stairs. A stunningly beautiful young woman delivered a file folder to him with a quick curtsy.

"You can shower while I read," Kingsley said.

"You're really going to make me take a shower?"

"I can give you a bath if you prefer."

"I wouldn't prefer," she said, not sure if she meant that.

Kingsley pushed open a set of intricately carved black double doors.

Never before had she seen a bedroom more erotic and inviting. She wished she knew more about architecture so she could properly describe it to her friends...if and when she ever made it out of here. She wanted to study the vaulted ceilings adorned with black-and-white paintings of lovers coupling in positions both pornographic and artistic. Or the hulking black marble fireplace and the lush oriental rugs covering the black-and-white tile floor.

But, in truth, it was the bed that held her attention. A huge four-poster behemoth, it captured both her attention and her imagination. She'd never seen sheets so red, like the color of fresh blood, or pillows so thick she thought she could drown in them and die happy.

"Nice bed," she said when Kingsley caught her staring. "It's really…big. King-size, I guess."

"Kingsley-sized." He winked at her as he pointed at a door across the room. "Bathroom in there. There is a bathrobe you can use while I have your clothes sent out."

Charlotte entered the bathroom and found it as luxurious as the bedroom. She locked the door behind her and looked in the mirror. Scuff marks had been only a slight exaggeration. A streak of black floor polish adorned her left cheek. It looked almost like a bruise. Her eyes were shaded with smudged and flaking eye makeup, her lipstick worn halfway off from the alcohol and the paraffin. She turned on the steam shower. As she washed the club grime off, she wondered what on earth

Kingsley wanted with her before deciding she didn't really care.

She turned off the water and wrapped herself in the plushest towel she'd ever felt in her life. Squeezing the water out of her hair, she pulled on the black silk bathrobe. With nothing on but the robe, she emerged into the bedroom. Kingsley reclined in a chair with his feet propped up on an ottoman. He had discarded his suit jacket and put on a pair of wire-rimmed glasses. Cocktail in hand, he perused the file folder.

"Hypocrite." She nodded at his cocktail and tried to ignore how desirable he looked in his embroidered vest with crisp white shirtsleeves rolled up to reveal muscular forearms.

"Everything in moderation, *ma chérie*. Except orgasms. Have a seat."

She didn't see anywhere to sit other than the bed and not wanting to seem too eager she sat on the floor. Kingsley gave her a strange look as she waited at his feet—a look both hungry and self-congratulatory.

Kingsley pulled out a sleek black cell phone. In rapid French, he poured out what sounded like instructions and hung up.

"Pancakes forthcoming. Now this is all very interesting." He flipped another page in the file. "You had a 4.0 at NYU before you dropped out your freshman year. *Pourquoi?*"

Charlotte sat up straighter. "That file's about me?" she demanded.

"*Oui.* While I was waiting for you to emerge from your Amaretto Sour coma, I had my secretary cull your records. You are a fascinating woman, Charlie."

"And you're such an asshole. I can't believe you're digging around my past."

"I intend to fuck you blind before you leave my home, Charlie. Is penetrating your past more intimate than penetrating your body?"

Charlotte closed her mouth and sat blushing on the floor as visions of Kingsley on top of her raced through her mind.

"I think so," she finally answered.

"So do I, actually."

"That's a pretty old-fashioned view of sex," she said. "Especially for a pimp."

"I am not a pimp. My employees do not sell sex. If I'm anything, it would be an agent. Or—"

"A talent scout," she finished. "Yeah, Steele told me. So were you scouting for talent at the club last night?"

"I was. And found a fire-breather. Not a

particularly useful talent but certainly interesting. As is this—your mother, she died when you were nineteen."

Charlotte swallowed. "Car accident. That's not interesting. Just horrible."

"Horrible, *très*. But you dropped out of school to raise your younger brother—that is interesting."

"Simon and my father do not get along. He was terrified at the prospect of living with my dad. We got a sympathetic judge, thank God."

Kingsley smiled at her over the top of his glasses. "Your father is not a good man?"

Charlotte pulled the robe tighter around her. "He's strict, conservative. I stayed out an hour past curfew when I was sixteen. I was at the movies with a girlfriend and we got ice cream after. He assumed the worst and called me a slut, a whore, everything. He and Mom divorced that year finally. I couldn't let Simon move in with him. Especially since—"

"Your brother is gay."

"Yeah, how did you know?"

"He interned with gay rights groups while in college and law school. You dropped out of university and started working so your gay brother wouldn't have to live with your conservative father. That's rather noble of you, Charlie."

Charlotte stared at the floor. "My dad would have destroyed Simon. It wasn't noble. It was my only choice."

"It wasn't, but it's quite telling that you think that. Let's see," he said and flipped a few more pages. "You worked as a receptionist at a salon after you quit school and apprenticed there. You were a cocktail waitress at Cirque de Nuit a few nights a week as well. Must have been before I bought the club. I would have remembered a fire-breather."

"You got much better tips if you could do a stunt. The bartender there before Steele taught me the fire-breathing thing."

"Your brother is in law school now. Full scholarship, I see. There's no reason you can't go back to school."

"I'm a little too old. Besides, I like working. I've been out in the real world taking care of myself and Simon since I was nineteen. Don't think I can go back."

Kingsley closed the file and leaned forward. He started to open his mouth but a knock on the door interrupted.

"*Entréz,*" he called out. The butler entered

carrying a breakfast tray. He sat it on the floor in front of Charlotte and quickly departed.

"So now you've had your shower and you are currently having your breakfast. Let's discuss the business opportunity you've already said no to."

"Discuss away," she said after her first delicious bite of pancake. "But it's still a no."

"Understandable." Kingsley stood up and removed his wire-rim glasses. "I'll talk. You eat."

"Happily."

Kingsley strolled leisurely about his bedroom. "I told you I was no pimp and that's true. There is a sexual aspect to the work my employees do, but none of them have sexual intercourse for money. At least not on my time clock. The clients we serve are an unusual lot with unusual desires. If they wanted mere sex, they could get that from their husbands and wives, boyfriends and girlfriends. What they want from us is more complicated."

"You're talking about kink, right?"

Kingsley nodded. "*Oui.* Kink. Bondage. Domination and sadomasochism. I said I was a talent agent. It wouldn't be far off the mark to also call myself a matchmaker. I have clients with specific desires, and I try to find a good match for those desires among my coterie. I have a client now—a wealthy businessman, not unattractive—who has found himself longing for a deeper connection than what he has experienced in his recent short-lived relationships. He prefers a beautiful woman somewhere between the age of twenty-five and thirty-five. No preference on race, height, or religion. Strong preference on intelligence—i.e. she must have it. And she must be brave."

At this last word, he turned around and looked down at her.

"A woman who breathes fire while drunk and comes to my home while sober is about as brave as this town has to offer. Wouldn't you agree, Charlie?"

Charlotte stared at him. She couldn't believe what he was asking her. "Okay…I'm not saying yes or anything. I'm only asking out of curiosity—what exactly would this whole arrangement entail?"

"This particular client enjoys S&M on occasion but is more interested in absolute sexual dominance. He is particularly aroused by fear."

"So he's a rapist?"

"Hardly. Dominants in the lifestyle, as we call it, find submission erotic. Overpowering a woman and taking her by force is an act of assault and violence. A dominant desires his submissive trust him enough to allow him to take her even when she is afraid. Yes, he takes but she gives as well. And you, *ma chérie,* have all the makings of a world-class submissive."

"This is bizarre."

"Is it? Tell me, Charlie, those two blond Barbie dolls you were with last night—that was Sasha Walsh and London Faber, yes?"

"Yes. We met at the salon. I cut their hair."

"Their parents are worth roughly the state budget of Vermont. They are vapid and dull and spoiled. They are your opposites. Why do you spend time with them?"

"Rich people are easy to hang out with. They have all the money. They make all the decisions."

"And they left you alone passed out on the floor of my club. Anything could have happened to you—you could have been robbed, assaulted.... They are not your friends."

"I know. That's why I like hanging out with them. It's easier that way."

"Easier to be with people who don't care about you?"

"Easier to be with people I don't have to care about. I know—it's stupid."

"*Pas du tout*. It's understandable. Your mother died, you raised your brother and kept him safe from your father...."

Charlotte toyed with the pancake left on her plate. *"Oui,"* she agreed.

"At a young age you had to take on enormous responsibilities. What you must understand is that submissive women are not weak. They are often much stronger than the men who dominate them. They have to be strong and brave to submit without losing themselves. I believe you are both. And," he said, squatting down in front of her, "I think there's a part of you that would very much enjoy not being in control of everything for once."

Charlotte looked up at him. No one that handsome should also be that insightful.

"I've never done kink before," she finally said.

"I can teach you everything you need to know."

"You would teach me?"

Kingsley tapped her under her chin and grinned at her. Something in his smile made her stomach clench. "Is that such a terrible prospect?"

Charlotte stared at him. Never before had she seen a more viscerally attractive man in her life. He seemed to read her reaction to him in her eyes.

The sane, rational part of Charlotte's brain told her to get up and get out. Unfortunately, every other part of her body and mind over-ruled her.

"Stand up," Kingsley ordered, and Charlotte came to her feet.

He looked her up and down once before flashing her a dangerous smile. Raising his hand, he caressed her lips with the soft pad of his thumb while he reached out with his free hand and opened a drawer on the bedside table. From it, he pulled a pair of handcuffs.

"Hey, no way in hell." Charlotte took a quick step back.

Kingsley said nothing as he slapped the cuffs onto his own left wrist.

"S'il vous plaît," he said and turned around, indicating he wanted her to cuff his hands behind his back.

Charlotte took the cuffs in her hand and nervously clapped them onto Kingsley's other wrist.

He turned around to face her. "Do you feel safe with me now?" he asked.

She nodded slowly. What could he really do to her with his hands cuffed, after all?

"Now," he said, "drop the robe."

Immediately, Charlotte pulled the robe tighter around her body.

"Charlie…take off the robe. Now."

Something in Kingsley's voice, some hard edge of authority, spoke to something deep within her. Slowly she untied the cord and let the robe fall to the floor. Kingsley ran his eyes up and down her body with an appraising air as she stood naked and blushing before him.

He stepped forward and she fought the urge to step back. Instead she stood her ground as he made a circuit around her body.

"You have exquisite breasts," he said. "The perfect size to fit in the palm of a large hand. I'm sure other lovers have told you that."

One old boyfriend had said she had "great tits," but that had been the extent of it.

"Not in so many words," she said.

"Pity. Also, lovely full hips. Well-rounded but with definition. Oh," he said pausing at her back. "You have a birthmark."

Every muscle in Charlotte's body tensed as Kingsley dropped to his knees behind her. "Just a little one."

"It looks like—" Kingsley's voice dropped to a low whisper "—the Eiffel Tower."

Charlotte laughed but the laugh turned to a

gasp when Kingsley's lips touched the birth-mark that graced the back of her left hip. The heat from his mouth on her skin spread through her entire pelvic region and sunk deep into her stomach. Just as the gasp started to turn to a low moan, Kingsley stood back up again.

"Long legs but not excessively so. Not too thin. Beautiful Celtic skin. Exquisite Roman nose."

"Roman? Is that a synonym for hooked?"

"*Oui.* You, Charlie, will do nicely."

"Um...*merci?*" she said, remembering one other French word.

"*De rien.* Now tell me...would you care to stay with me? One month. Let me train you to be the perfect sexual submissive."

"I have a job, you know." She grabbed the robe off the floor and pulled it around her again.

"I'll pay you twice what you made in your best month last year. Cash. Of course."

"Of course." Charlotte swallowed. Good Lord, he really meant it. This drop-dead gor-geous, rich, weird Frenchman wanted her to stay with him for a month. And not just stay with him; he wanted to teach her how to submit sexually to some rich client of his. Insanity. And yet, the thought of walking away from this offer.... No, that wasn't right. The thought of walking away from *him*....

She couldn't do it. She couldn't walk away from Kingsley.

"I'm not agreeing to anything," she finally said. "I haven't even met this guy."

"I won't ask you to agree to anything until you meet him. Nor will he agree to anything until he's met you. We'll spend the next few weeks in training. When you're ready, I'll arrange a meeting. If you like each other and decide to give a relationship a try, he'll pay me my rather exorbitant finder's fee and you and he can work out whatever financial arrangement best suits you both. Knowing him, he'll offer you a room in his rather impressive home and the freedom to come and go as you please as long as you are at his disposal three to five evenings a week. He'll have a partner who is his sexual equal, and you'll have someone who is quite happy to make most or all of the decisions so you, for once in your life, won't have to."

"My feminist friends would kill me."

"Those of us in the lifestyle are too busy having good sex to worry about the gender wars. True, most submissives are women and most dominants men. But I have several male submissives on my payroll, and I know every dominatrix in this town. I assure you the vast majority of my clients are men who want to be dominated by women. So you needn't worry that you're giving up your right to vote or right to equal pay. You're only giving up boring vanilla sex, and I promise you, you won't miss it. Say yes, Charlie. We know you want to."

"Okay...yes. Fine. I want to."

"Beautiful, brave, and honest—I may have to keep you. You can stay in the room next to mine. I'll send my secretary to see you have everything you need. In the meantime, I'm afraid I have to behave myself and get some actual work done today."

Charlotte took a slow, deep breath. "Okay, I'll stay for a few days. Maybe a month. I've been trying to take a vacation for two years."

Kingsley turned his head and smiled at her with a cocked eyebrow. "*Ma chérie*...this will be no vacation."

And then he laughed and something in that laugh caused her toes to curl and dig into the rug under her feet. The laugh rippled up her body and wrapped around her hips and dug like fingers into her stomach.

"Right...." she said, suddenly very aware of her nakedness under the bathrobe. Knowing Kingsley still had the handcuffs on his wrists came as both a relief and a disappointment. "I should go and let you get to work, I guess."

Charlotte started for the door but stopped before leaving. "I should probably take those off you," she said, remembering the handcuffs.

Gasping, Charlotte found herself with her back pressed to the door and Kingsley's arms imprisoning her on either side. The handcuffs dangled impotently off his right wrist.

"*Pas de problème*, Charlie. Anything that needs taking off...I will do it."

At first, fear alone kept Charlotte frozen to the door. She sensed the iron strength in Kingsley's arms, in his body, that had her trapped in place. Kingsley pushed forward until his hips pressed into her hips, his chest into her breasts, and the fear turned to another feeling equally powerful but no less terrifying.

"Let me go," she whispered.

"*Non*. Not yet." Kingsley caressed the right side of her face with his fingertips. "You're here to learn. This is your first lesson. The man I'll train you for enjoys games like this...games of passion and fear. He will want you ready for him always. In the middle of the night he might wake you with his hunger. He may find you reading in the evening and without a word take your book from you and your clothes. You will try to pass him in the hallway, and he will stop you with his arms, turn you around, press you to the wall and force himself inside you. *Comprende?*"

Charlotte swallowed hard. "So this is the lesson? Learning to keep my mouth shut while he does whatever he wants to me?"

Kingsley shook his head. He slid his hand from her face and down the front of her body. She inhaled as Kingsley cupped her left breast and gently kneaded her nipple with his thumb and forefinger.

"The lesson is that you must learn to speak when he does something you do not want him to do. Do you know what a safe word is, Charlie? We use them in my world."

"No," she breathed as liquid need began to gather in her hips.

"It's a word, any word, that the two parties involved agree upon. It is the word that you must use to stop whatever is happening to you that you don't want."

"I can't say 'no'?"

"For this man I will train you for,"

Kingsley said as he moved his hand lower over her quivering stomach, "the word 'no' gasped in fear, in protest, will only stoke his passion further. It is a game, you see. The more you resist, the more he will desire you. Say 'no' and he will carry on. Say 'stop' and he will not stop. Say 'don't' if you wish, but he will do whatever he will do."

Kingsley shifted his hand from her stomach to between her legs. "Tell me to stop," he said. "I dare you."

"Stop it," she whispered, although she didn't mean it.

"Stop what? This?" Kingsley's middle finger slipped inside her. Closing her eyes tight, Charlotte thrust her hips out and into Kingsley's hand.

"Yes," she replied, panting. "Stop…that."

"Should I stop this, too?" He pushed a second finger into her and began to move his hand, thrusting in and out of her with his fingers.

Charlotte nodded, unable to speak from the sheer pleasure of his touch. She sensed Kingsley's mouth at her ear.

"*Non,*" he said again. "I'm enjoying myself too much to stop. You feel exquisite inside. So warm, so wet…did you know if I touch right here—" Kingsley twisted his hand and pressed the tip of his finger hard and deep into a spot one inch inside her "—I can feel your pulse?"

"Kingsley…." His name was the only word Charlotte could push past her lips. He apparently took it as an encouragement, because a third finger joined the second and Charlotte had to open her legs wider to take it.

"Now pretend for a moment that you aren't actually enjoying this as much as we both know you are," Kingsley said, making lazy circles with his hand inside her. "Shocking thought, *oui?*"

"*Oui,*" Charlotte agreed. She truly couldn't remember the last time she'd felt anything so erotic. The expertise of his technique, the pressure, the movements were beyond pleasurable. Far more erotic, however, was the power of the man who held her pressed to the door and refused to let her go even as she mock-protested.

"Let us say you really did want me to stop. Except, as I've demonstrated, we both know when you say 'stop' in this context, you don't really mean it. Not with me. So you need a word that truly means stop, and to that alone will I listen. That is your safe word. Do you understand?"

"I think so." Charlotte grasped his left forearm and held onto him as she felt her climax building. Hungover...scared...in a stranger's house...and yet she could scarcely breathe for her desire. "So what's my safe word?"

The muscles deep inside her tightened around Kingsley's hand. She felt a rush of wetness between her thighs.

"As you are my little red-headed fire-breather, your safe word should be 'dragon.' You must say it whenever you truly wish me to stop whatever I'm doing. No other word, no amount of struggling will do it."

Charlotte's breathing turned hard and heavy as Kingsley's hand moved faster and deeper into her. His thumb massaged her clitoris. Never before had she been with a man who knew how to manipulate a woman's body so well.

With his lips, Kingsley traced a path from Charlotte's ear to her shoulder. Charlotte dug her fingernails into the fabric of his jacket.

"So if you truly wish me to stop what I'm doing, Charlie, you will say...?"

"Dragon."

Kingsley pulled his hand abruptly out of her body and took a step back. Charlotte nearly collapsed from the sudden shock of his departure as her vaginal muscles fluttered in protest.

"*C'est ça,*" Kingsley said. "It's like magic."

Kingsley took her hand and kissed the back of it. "Get settled in," he said. "I'm off to work now. No rest for the wicked."

Kingsley pulled her away from the door, opened it and strolled into the hall whistling a song she thought might have been the French national anthem.

Charlotte closed her eyes and imagined fire shooting out of her mouth and burning Kingsley to the ground. She must have actually audibly hissed because Kingsley stopped whistling long enough to call back to her.

"Patience, Charlie. We have all month."

❦

CHARLOTTE SPENT the rest of the afternoon in the bedroom Kingsley had assigned to her, a bedroom nearly as luxurious as his own. His secretary came in and gathered information from her—emergency contacts, food preferences, even allergies.

"Allergies?" Charlotte had asked, repeating the woman's question.

"Latex, for example?" Kingsley's secretary answered with hardly a blink or a blush.

"Oh, God."

An hour after returning from her apartment with a month's worth of clothes and supplies, Charlotte tried to get some sleep but her mind wanted to wander down far too many dangerous paths. Kingsley Edge…. The one and only Kingsley Edge. She finally worked up the courage to call her younger brother and let him know a little of what was going on.

Simon sighed heavily, so heavily Charlotte nearly laughed aloud. "You sure about this, Char?" he asked.

"I like him."

"Do you like him because he rich and infamous or because you actually like him?"

Charlotte thought about the question, a perfectly valid one, for a few seconds before answering.

"Yes."

After getting Simon's blessing, or at least his promise to not call the police, Charlotte hung up and stared around the room still not quite believing she'd be spending the next month here. What would Kingsley do with her during her stay? Part of her was terrified at the prospect. Another much bigger part of her couldn't wait to find out.

Charlotte started as an envelope slipped in under her door. She picked it up and found a hand-written invitation.

Charlie—Present yourself at my bedroom door this evening at nine o'clock. Wear your finest. We shall attend a piano recital in the music room. Do not be late. The consequences will be both severe and enjoyable if you are.

Charlotte corrected herself. Invitation? No, this was a summons. And although she knew she should bristle at the order to present herself on time or be punished, she almost wanted to be late simply to force Kingsley to make good on his threat.

For a solid hour, Charlotte stood before the bathroom mirror primping for the recital. She did her makeup quickly and spent the rest of the time curling her waist-length hair into thick red waves. The fanciest dress she had was a little black number. Hopefully the effect of her hair would distract Kingsley from the simplicity of the dress.

At nine on the dot, Charlotte was outside Kingsley's bedroom door, waiting on him to answer her knock. She still barely knew the man. The more time that passed from their one long conversation this morning, the more she questioned her decision to stay with him for the month. This was crazy, right? Spending a month with a stranger? No one in her right mind would have agreed to his offer. Why was she doing this?

Kingsley opened the door.

Okay, that was why.

"Wow," she said when all other words failed her.

He wore a black suit with silver buttons on the black-and-silver embroidered vest. His riding boots had been polished to a near-reflective shine. Had she stared into those boots long enough, she imagined she would have seen her own wide-eyed face staring back at her.

"You approve?" Kingsley asked, a slight smile at the corner of his sensual lips.

Charlotte slowly nodded. "Um…yes. You look…damn."

"And you, *ma chérie*, look enchanting." Kingsley took her hand and kissed the back of it. "Utterly exquisite." Raising her hand over her head, he spun her in a slow circle. "*Parfait*, Charlie."

"Merci," she said and curtsied. "The dress isn't much. But it's all I have that's semiformal."

Kingsley took her by the arm and they started down the hallway. "It will look lovely on the floor by my bed."

Charlotte blushed and laughed. "Is there any particular reason why you dress like it's the nineteenth century instead of the twenty-first?"

"There's only one reason that matters," he said as he escorted her down to the main level of his home. "Because I can."

He led her to the music room. Kingsley introduced her, still on his arm, to his guests. Most of the men were seated on the chairs and loveseats. But although there was enough room for all, a few of the women sat on the floor at the feet of the men they'd come with. One woman, almost forty and stunningly beautiful, took an imperious seat on a chair and snapped her fingers. Her date, a young man of about thirty, swiftly sat down at her feet.

Kingsley had a wicked gleam in his eyes as he observed Charlotte take in the scene. When he settled down, she instinctively sank to the floor and leaned back against his knee. He ran a hand possessively through her hair. Now she knew why no one had asked her how she'd met Kingsley. All his guests were part of his kinky little community.

Charlotte adjusted herself and found the floor was actually quite comfortable. The carpeting was thick and lush and Kingsley's fingers in her hair and on her neck felt extraordinary—sensual and seductive and also relaxing. She could stay here all night.

A tall blond man entered to a smattering of applause and sat at the piano. Charlotte's eyes widened when she saw he was dressed like a priest. A beautiful young woman with black hair followed him and sat on the floor next to the piano bench. Once the applause ceased, the man began to play. Charlotte sat still, entranced by the breathtakingly handsome pianist and the woman who rested so contentedly at his feet.

Kingsley leaned forward and put his mouth at her ear. "I know he's handsome as the devil, Charlie. And you're welcome to look all you want. But don't touch. That," he said, inclining his head toward the piano playing priest and the young woman, "is a love match."

"A love match?" she asked. "One of yours?"

"Oh, no. Destiny brought those two together. I had nothing to do with it. When destiny fails, that's when I get called."

"You should put that on your business cards," she joked.

Kingsley reached into his pocket and handed her a black business card embossed with silver lettering. "Kingsley Edge, CEO, Edge Enterprises. *When destiny fails…*" it read.

She covered her mouth to stop herself from laughing out loud as she looked up at Kingsley. He was smiling at her. It wasn't a normal smile of mirth or pleasure, but a smile that sent her body temperature and heart rate soaring.

Charlotte turned away and tried to let the music calm her down. But it was such passionate music played so skillfully that Charlotte felt it wanted to seduce her as much as Kingsley. And both were succeeding. By the time the recital ended, Charlotte was so desperate for Kingsley that she pretended to stumble when standing just so she could lean her full weight against him. He pulled her close to him, and she inhaled his scent. He smelled warm and masculine. Every nerve in her body sat on edge at his nearness. When he bade his guests a swift goodbye and escorted her back upstairs, she was nearly shaking with eagerness. They stopped at the door to her room.

"So he's really a priest?" she asked. "The pianist?"

"I told you I had a priest on speed dial. You really should learn to trust me."

"I'm trying. This is all new."

Kingsley laid his hand on her neck and rested his thumb at the hollow of her throat. "I will not hurt you, Charlie. Or at least I won't harm you," he said with a roguish grin. "Do you believe that? We won't get very far until you know that the moment you are most afraid of me, it is the moment you have the least reason to be."

"Okay, I'll try not to be afraid."

"You can be afraid all you want. Just don't let your fear stop you."

Charlotte inhaled. For whatever reason, she did trust him.

"Good girl," he said, taking her hand. He kissed it slowly and let it go. "Good night, Charlie."

She stared at him as he strode toward his own bedroom.

Stunned that he'd left her, Charlotte entered her bedroom on feet of lead. Hurt and embarrassed, she considered gathering her things and getting out of this madhouse. He'd spent all evening seducing her with every glance, every touch and every smile. And now he just sauntered off to bed, leaving her alone in her room.

She took a deep breath and remembered his words—*you really should learn to trust me.* Maybe this was a test. Maybe he was seeing if she would get pissed and try to leave.

Charlotte kicked off her shoes and enjoyed the sound of them bouncing hollowly off the wall. She'd give this weird place one more day. But she couldn't completely talk herself out of her disappointment and frustration. Kingsley knew she was more than ready and willing to go to bed with him. Maybe he got off on being a tease. Maybe when he finally did invite her to his room, she'd kiss his hand and walk off like he had.

In the bathroom, she brushed her teeth and glanced at herself in the mirror. Kingsley had called her beautiful, but she never really thought she was. Pretty, maybe. Not beautiful. Tonight with her hair flowing like red wine down her back, she knew she'd never looked better. But that hadn't been good enough for him. Angry, she strode back into the bedroom.

Charlotte froze when she sensed something

behind her. Suddenly, she couldn't move as two incredibly strong arms grabbed her and held her hard and fast in place, a hand covering her mouth. She threw all of her strength into her struggle to get loose but the harder she fought the harder he held her.

"Shh…." Kingsley's mouth was at her ear again. "It's only me."

Knowing it was Kingsley didn't do anything to calm her fears. She tried to pull away again but still he held her tight against him. She screamed against his hand. Barely a sound came out.

"Charlie, I know you're afraid right now. You are allowed to be afraid. I want you to be afraid." His voice was low and intimate. She pushed back against him, hoping to knock him off balance and get away. But he was too tall, too strong. She turned her head trying to scream, but his hand was a vise over her mouth. "In the lifestyle, we all have a safe word. It's the word you say when you want the game to stop. Your safe word is 'dragon' since you're my little red-headed fire-breather. And the second I take my hand away, you can say 'dragon' and I'll let you go. Or…or you can choose to not fear your fear. Vanilla sex is all about trust. Rape is all about fear. In that place between fear and trust is where we live. Trust me, Charlie. Don't think that the fear means you have to stop."

Charlotte closed her eyes. She wrenched herself to the side, but still she couldn't get free from him.

"I'm going to move my hand away from your mouth now. Say your safe word if you must. But before you do, ask yourself how you felt when I walked away from you tonight. Ask yourself how you will feel tomorrow if you walk away from me now."

Charlotte panted against his palm. He slowly took his hand away from her mouth. She started to speak and then swallowed her words.

She heard Kingsley's smug laugh at her ear. "I have good taste in women, don't I?"

Charlotte opened her mouth to argue but Kingsley pushed her hard and bent her over the bed. He took her arms and yanked them behind her back and pinned them there. With one hand, he held her wrists; with the other, he reached underneath her dress. He ran his hand up the back of her thighs and slid it over her hips and into her panties.

"Your clit's swollen and you're soaking wet," he said as he examined her. She clenched her jaw but was too humiliated to say any-thing. His fingers skimmed across the outside of her body. She flinched as he ripped her flimsy panties off her with a quick tear. Now naked underneath her dress, there was nothing between him and her. Kingsley used his knees to push her legs wider apart. His hand came back to her and she groaned as he slid a single finger inside her.

"Since the moment I saw you breathing fire at my club last night," Kingsley whispered as one finger became two, and two fingers turned to three inside her, "I knew I had to have you…to feel that fire inside you."

He pulled his hand roughly out of her, leaving her scared and panting against the sheets.

"Don't move," he ordered. Closing her eyes, she dug her hands into the sheets and tried to breathe through her fear.

"It's adrenaline," Kingsley said as he opened a drawer and pulled something out, something that sounded like metal. She gasped as he took her wrists again and yanked them behind her back. "What you're feeling right now—it isn't fear. You aren't afraid of me. You've simply never been this excited before."

"God, you're arrogant," Charlotte growled

as Kingsley slapped cold metal handcuffs on each of her wrists.

"I'm not arrogant, I'm French." He forced her legs apart again as Charlotte tried to relax into the handcuffs. The weight of the cold metal dug into her skin. She felt helpless, hopeless. One word could get her out of this. All she had to do was say it and Kingsley would let her go.

But she couldn't say it. Even scared and humiliated, she couldn't deny that she wanted him, wanted this so much it scared her more than the handcuffs and the man who had taken possession of her body.

He cleared his throat. "Now, Charlie, I'm going to put my cock in you in two seconds. If you have an objection to that, I would raise it right now."

Charlotte said nothing as hot tears of shame welled up in her eyes.

"I thought as much," he said and shoved inside her.

He was so big it almost hurt going in. She strained against the handcuffs and pressed her face into the bed as Kingsley thrust into her with strokes both hard and slow. Reaching around her hips, he found her clitoris again. With an expert touch he teased it until Charlotte cried out. As her orgasm peaked and waned, Kingsley roughly turned her onto her back and pushed her legs open again.

Kingsley yanked her dress down and bared her breasts. His mouth dropped to her neck. He rained violent kisses across her chest and shoulders so roughly she knew she'd have bruises from his mouth tomorrow. He took both breasts in his hands and held them as he penetrated her again. She opened her legs wider and took him as deeply into her body as she could.

Bending over her, he met her eye-to-eye. "You tilt your hips high. You like deep penetration, don't you?" Charlotte turned her head and stared at the wall. But Kingsley grabbed her face again and forced her to look at him. "Answer me."

"Yes," she said. "I like it deep."

"Then by all means." Kingsley grabbed her knees and wrenched them up and over his shoulders. She arched back—each thrust seemed to pound at the base of her stomach.

Charlotte panted as Kingsley continued his assault on her. She hated how good it felt being taken like this, hated herself for liking the brutality so much. He manipulated her body like he owned it, touched her like her body was an open book he'd read and memorized. Turning her head, Charlotte pressed her face to her arm. As Kingsley kneaded her clitoris between his thumb and forefinger, she came so hard that tears rolled out of the corners of her eyes.

Kingsley lowered her legs off his shoulders and covered her body with his. Instinctively Charlotte wrapped her legs around his waist as he continued to move in her. He bit her neck, her collarbone, kissed the hollow of her throat all while still moving in her.

"You like this," he said.

"Yes," she whispered as she flinched at a particularly hard thrust.

"Call me 'sir' when I'm inside you, Charlie."

"Yes, sir," she breathed, wanting to both kiss him and slap him the second her hands were free.

She kept waiting for him to be done with her. But there seemed to be no end to the pleasure he inflicted on her. He pushed and pushed until Charlotte felt her inner muscles start to tighten. Raising her hips, she took him deep into her again. She closed her eyes as another orgasm ripped through her. Finally, Kingsley's movements grew harsher and faster. His fingers dug into the back of her neck. He held her still, forcing her to meet his eyes. With one last, brutal thrust, he came with his eyes open and locked onto hers.

Still inside her, he moved her legs flat on her bed. Her body continued to pulse around his length as his cock pulsed inside her. He dipped his head and for the first time since meeting, kissed her.

She opened her mouth to his and his tongue slipped inside. His kiss—gentle and subtle—was the opposite of the sex. She wanted him to stay in her mouth and her body all night. Kingsley pulled back and smiled down at her.

"Took you long enough to kiss me, sir," she said, remembering his orders, remembering he was still inside her.

"You're a fire-breather, Charlie. You can't blame me for being wary of your mouth."

She laughed a little but winced as he pulled out of her sore body. She lay on her back, letting her heart slow its frenetic beating as he disappeared into the bathroom. She wondered what she looked like. Her dress was torn and still bunched around her stomach. She could already tell she was covered in bruises from his hands and his mouth. Even inside she felt bruised from his merciless thrusts.

Kingsley emerged and stood by the bed. He looked immaculate in his suit. He'd been fully dressed when he'd taken her, and had only removed his shoes, socks, and jacket. He reached into his pocket and pulled out the handcuff key and released her. She rolled up and tried to straighten her dress.

"What?" she asked as Kingsley stared at her.

"You look beautiful."

"I look like I've been assaulted." She wiped her eyes and a smudge of eyeliner came off on her fingers.

"You look like a woman who's been ravished and thoroughly enjoyed it."

"You scared the shit out of me grabbing me like that."

Kingsley sat on the bed next to her. "You like being scared."

Charlotte didn't answer. Kingsley took her by the chin again, this time gently. He caressed her bottom lip with his thumb. "You like being scared," he repeated. "You don't have to be afraid of your fear, Charlie. You're allowed to be afraid and like it."

"Normal people aren't supposed to like this

stuff. Normal people aren't supposed to enjoy being thrown down, tied up, and practically taken against their will."

"My beautiful Charlie." Kingsley kissed her slowly. "Perhaps it's time to admit you aren't normal people."

❦

CHARLOTTE WOKE EARLY the next morning. She put on the black bathrobe and found his bedroom door ajar, but no King.

After eating breakfast in his opulent kitchen, she wandered back upstairs to shower and dress. When she stepped out of the shower, she found Kingsley standing there waiting with a towel.

"You're trying to kill me," she said as she snatched the towel out of his hands. "Give me a little warning, please, if you're going to shower-stalk me."

"You must learn to keep on your toes. Come here, Charlie. Let's see the damage, shall we?"

Charlotte stepped out of the shower. Kingsley stood in front of her and unwrapped her towel. Even though they'd had the most intense sex of her life last night, he hadn't actually seen her completely naked. Just standing there in front of him was embarrassing and awkward. He, of course, seemed slightly aroused and amused as always.

"How bad is it?"

"Terrible. I barely left a mark on you. We'll have to rectify that."

"What do you call these?"

She pointed to the bruises on her chest and shoulders.

"Just nibbles." Kingsley bit her wet neck.

"This isn't fair, you know." She wrapped her arms over her bare breasts. "I haven't gotten to see you naked yet."

"Women tend to fall in love with me when I take my clothes off."

"You're a narcissist. Come on—just a peek?"

Kingsley arched an eyebrow at her. "Very well. If you insist."

He strode from the bathroom. Grabbing her towel, Charlotte followed him into his bedroom.

She stood in the center of his room while he started to undress. Today's look was more Edwardian than Victorian. His jacket had five buttons and she watched with eager anticipation as he brusquely undid all of them. Tossing the jacket aside, he unknotted his tie and pulled his white shirt from his trousers. She gasped when he shed the shirt and stood bare-chested in front of her.

"Oh, my God." Charlotte covered her mouth in shock.

"You were warned."

She reached out and tentatively touched his chest. His body was what she imagined—lean and muscled and tan. But she never imagined this.

"How?" She looked up at his eyes.

"I was in the French Foreign Legion in my early twenties. Bullet wounds."

"You were shot."

"Four times. Thankfully all were small-caliber and missed vital organs. Especially my favorite vital organ."

Charlotte tried to laugh but it wasn't easy staring at the four small holes that riddled Kingsley's stomach and chest. "Was this from a battle?"

"Two are from a skirmish. The other two are friendly fire."

"Friendly fire?"

Kingsley grinned at her. "Not terribly friendly, really. My CO found me with his wife."

Now Charlotte did laugh. "Then you deserved it."

"Hardly. That poor woman was begging to be tied up and defiled. Literally—she begged me."

"You've always been this bad?" she asked as she ran her hand up and down his bare chest.

"*Au contraire*. I've always been this good."

Kingsley took her by the wrists and led her to his bed. He opened the drawer of the bedside table and pulled out a length of rope.

"Have you ever been hit by a man, Charlie?" Kingsley asked as he pulled the towel off her and threw it aside.

"No. Dad yelled but he never hit."

"And your boyfriends? Never even spanked?"

She shook her head as her heart started racing. Was he going to actually hit her?

"Your lovers have been vanilla," Kingsley said. "That's a tragedy. Did you even enjoy fucking them?"

She shrugged her shoulders. "They were nice. I had orgasms. It wasn't terrible. Just—"

"Boring? Unfulfilling? *Bourgeois?*"

"All of that, I guess. Simon told me I was

crazy to keep dumping such great guys. He said he'd take them if I didn't want them."

Kingsley took Charlotte's wrists and tied them high on the bedpost. Water from her shower ran down her back and her legs all the way to her ankles. The water droplets itched and tickled but she couldn't reach down to wipe them off.

"You would have been crazy to stay with men who didn't understand you. Compromise is one thing. Denying your true self is another. Now…" He stood behind her. "I'm going to do something to you that is neither boring nor *bourgeois*. I'm going to flog you for five minutes. And if you make it through those five minutes without saying your safe word, I'll give you an orgasm. And then I will flog you for eight minutes. And then I will give you another orgasm. And so on and so on. I'll add three minutes to each beating. And the game only ends when you safe out."

"What if I don't safe out?"

"Then we'll be here for a very long time," he whispered into her ear. "Because there's nothing in the world I enjoy more than beating a beautiful woman and then bringing her to climax. Now where did I put that cat?"

"Cat? You have a cat?"

"Cat of nine tails, Charlie. Now be a good girl and just stay put while I find a few things."

Charlotte was fairly certain Kingsley knew exactly where everything was. He just wanted to leave her tied up naked and waiting, letting the anticipation scare her. She heard what sounded like a trunk opening and then she felt him standing behind her again. Something landed with a thump on the bed. It was brown leather with a six-inch handle and nine leather thongs. It didn't look terrifying…but it didn't look fun, either. A tube of lubricant landed beside it. One more thud, louder than the others, heralded the arrival of an impressive-looking vibrator.

Kingsley brought his hand around and waved a stopwatch in front of her face. "Five minutes." He set the alarm. "Ready?"

"Yes, sir."

"You're trying to get me to fuck you by calling me 'sir,' aren't you? It will work. But not yet."

Before she could say anything else, the flogger was off the bed and he'd landed the first blow on her back. She flinched at the sudden burning pain. It was shockingly sharp, but not unbearable. She breathed through her nose in short, desperate bursts. She was determined to not to say her safe word. It wasn't so much that she wanted the orgasm. She wanted to prove to Kingsley she wasn't boring.

When she heard the chiming of the stopwatch alarm, she sagged with relief. Kingsley pressed his bare chest into her burning back. The flogger landed on his bed again.

"Did you enjoy that, Charlie?"

"No," she said, still panting.

"Good. I hate beating masochists. They take the fun out of it by actually enjoying the pain."

"I'm letting you do this to me," she said between breaths. "I'm not a masochist?"

"Oh, no, Charlie. You're not a masochist. You're a slut."

"I am not—"

He hushed her before she could finish her angry protest. "Charlie, in this house, the word *slut* is the highest compliment I can give. It means you are a person who owns her sexuality and is unafraid to experiment and open her mind and body to new experiences. I'm a slut, too."

"I've noticed."

"Now that you've had your pain, I suppose you'll be wanting your pleasure."

Kingsley reached out for the lubricant and

opened the tube. He slid his hand between her legs and applied a generous dose to her labia. She shivered from the cold and the wet, but relished the pleasure his dexterous fingers were giving her.

"I know I was a little rough on you last night. But I can be merciful."

He took the vibrator and turned it on. He moved Charlotte's legs apart and slid it slowly into her. She inhaled as it went deep inside her. Her body slowly stretched to take it all in.

"This is merciful?" she asked.

"It's not as big as I am."

He moved it in and out of her slowly as his fingers found her clitoris and teased it. The vibrator did its work quickly. She cried out as her body spasmed around it and against Kingsley's hand. He pulled it out of her and laid it on the bed again.

"I'll give you another one in eight minutes," he whispered into her ear. Again he set the alarm on the stopwatch. Her body was still twitching with pleasure when the flogger struck her sore back. She concentrated on her waning pleasure and tried to ignore the growing pain.

She found that if she opened her back instead of clenching her muscles, the agony was flatter, less acute. Her head fell back. She stared up at the ceiling. After a few minutes she barely felt anything at all.

A chiming sound jarred her from her trance.

Kingsley picked up the vibrator again and pressed the tip against her clitoris. She gasped from the shock of pleasure. She'd never been with a man who understood how to manipulate a woman's body so well. The pressure on her clitoris was perfect. His fingers inside her found all her sensitive spots. He seemed far more concerned with her orgasms than his. She couldn't believe what she was thinking. She was tied to a bedpost for a flogging and all she could think about was how good he made her feel.

Charlotte's orgasm spiked into her stomach and she almost wrenched her shoulder from how hard she flinched.

"If you can take eleven minutes of beating, then I'll fuck you again," Kingsley whispered into her ear. "How does that sound?"

"Very good."

Kingsley slapped her hard on her right thigh.

"I mean, very good, sir."

By now, Charlotte knew how to handle

this. She closed her eyes and let the pain roll over her and off her. In her mind she was somewhere else. In her mind she was untied and on her back with Kingsley on top of her and deep inside her....

Before she knew it, she heard the beeping of the stopwatch alarm again. "Thank God," she breathed with relief. Another minute and she would have given in.

"You're welcome."

Kingsley threw the flogger on the bed. Standing behind her, he ran his hands up and down the front of her body. He stopped at her breasts. He teased her nipples until they were hard and sore. He kissed her neck and shoulder.

"Tell me the truth, Charlie. Have you ever been taken here?" He ran his hand over her bottom.

"You mean anal?" she asked. "Once."

"Did you like it?"

"Undecided."

"That's because you've never had it with me. Let's rectify that, shall we?"

She wasn't sure she wanted this, but she knew she didn't want to stop him, either. Her heart fluttered in fear. But she remembered

Kingsley's admonitions and didn't let the fear stop her.

He applied more lubricant to her. She sighed at how good the cold, wet liquid felt going into her. Kingsley took his time preparing her body. She tried to relax. As big as he was, she would have to be very relaxed to take him inside her.

King pressed close to her. She closed her eyes when she felt him start to push into her. He grabbed her thigh and lifted it. She rested her knee on top of the bed. Slowly he entered her inch by inch. Last night he'd been shockingly brutal with her. Now he was nothing but careful. She shivered at how strangely good it felt to have him inside her this way. Kingsley moved in and out of her with gentle, careful thrusts.

With her eyes still closed, she didn't notice that Kingsley had picked up the vibrator again. But when he started to push it inside her, she opened her eyes in shock.

"Breathe, Charlie. You can take both." He pushed the vibrator all the way into her as he continued his slow thrusts from behind. "You've never been penetrated anally and vaginally at the same time before?"

"No...never."

"My poor girl. You were practically a virgin." She heard his smug laugh at her ear.

He continued to thrust into her. Charlotte moved her hips in rhythm with Kingsley's. She climaxed quickly around the vibrator. The sensations were so intense they were almost painful. After her second orgasm, he finally pulled the vibrator out.

Kingsley gripped her by the hips and thrust faster. She was nearly insensate from the two intense orgasms he'd given her. She simply hung from her bonds as he fucked her.

She winced as his fingers tightened their hold. He pushed hard into her and came with a ragged breath.

He pulled out slowly. A minute later he came back to the bed. Charlotte saw him reach for the flogger.

"Dragon," she said, finally.

He dropped the flogger as if he'd been struck, and reached up and untied her. She collapsed back into his arms.

He picked her up and laid her down. Kneeling on the floor next to the bed, he ran a hand through her still wet hair. He didn't seem the least upset with her that she'd stopped him.

"Too much pain, *ma chérie*?" Kinigsley asked.

"No." She shook her head and smiled tiredly at him. The muscles inside her still fluttered. "Too much pleasure."

❧

THE NEXT FEW weeks at *Chez Kingsley* passed in a haze of sex and pain and more sex. Kingsley was a near limitless font of alternative sexual knowledge and experience. He introduced her to something new every day. One day it was nipple clamps. The next day spanking. He taught her to beg for his cock. Taught her to crawl for him. One day he dressed in leather pants and whipped her. The next day he put her in lingerie, tied her to his bed with silk scarves, and violated her every orifice. Last weekend he'd even videotaped them having sex and made her watch it. Then he'd given her the only copy of the tape and let her decide what to do with it. Her first instinct was to destroy it.

She hadn't.

And every few days when she least suspected it, when she was certain he was out of the house or in a meeting, he would sneak up on her, grab her, throw her against the wall or push her onto the floor or the bed and ravish her with shocking brutality. No matter how many times he did this, it always terrified her. And no matter the pain involved, she always loved it.

Tonight, his plans for her were maddeningly opaque. He'd ordered her to wait naked in his bedroom in his huge chaise longue armchair. She leaned back into the plush fabric and closed her eyes. The chair was nearly the size of a love seat. He'd taken her a few times on it already. The chair arms were the perfect place for her legs to drape over as he thrust into her. She only had one more week here with Kingsley before she met the client he'd been training her for. She didn't think she'd be able to run off with this guy no matter how rich and "not unattractive" he was. Still…she also couldn't imagine leaving this place and returning entirely to her old life. Kingsley had marked her and not just with the bruises on her body.

She did miss work, however, and would be glad to go back to it. She'd cut everyone's hair in Kingsley's household except for Kingsley himself. He told her no one but his barber in France was allowed near his hair. She called him a coward and he'd punished her in wicked ways for the insult.

"You've got a lovely smile on your lips, Charlie. I'd love to know if I put it there."

Opening her eyes, she found Kingsley standing above her. "I was thinking about what I'd do to your hair if you let me cut it. Your hot mess is very dashing, but I could make it even better."

"You come near me with your scissors, and I'll make sure you wake up with significantly less hair in the morning."

Charlotte laughed. He'd shaved her in the bath last night. If he had no compunction about removing her most private hair, she knew he wouldn't hesitate to cut any other hair off.

"Fine. I'll leave your hair alone. But you keep telling me I have to trust you. When are you going to start trusting me a little?"

"I trust you quite a bit. Just not with my hair. But I'm glad you mention trust."

He held up a black scarf.

"Blindfold?" she guessed.

"*Très bien, ma chérie.*"

Everything Kingsley had done to her, he'd done with her eyes open. The blindfold made her nervous; she could tell from the smile on his face that he was enjoying that fact.

He tied it around her eyes and the room went completely dark.

She started when Kingsley took her ankles and pushed her legs wide open and draped them over the arms of the chair. She heard him pull the ottoman close. She knew he was sitting on it in front of her exposed body. A month ago she would have been mortified, but no longer. Kingsley had taught her to be shameless. She was enjoying shameless. She hadn't even gone out drinking or clubbing since she met Kingsley. He was all the decadence she needed.

"Let's play a guessing game, Charlie. You guess all five right and you can do anything you want to me when the game is over."

"Anything?"

"Anything that isn't illegal. Or at least anything we won't get caught doing."

"What am I guessing?"

"You're guessing what object I'm putting inside you."

All her self-congratulatory anti-shame thoughts went out the window. "You are going to stick stuff in me, and I have to guess what it is?"

"I think I just said that. Ready?"

"No," she said but didn't safe out. She'd

quickly learned with Kingsley that "no" meant anything but "no" to him. Until she said "dragon," she was in.

She felt Kingsley's fingertips opening her up. And then something slightly flat pushed slowly into her. It had a round base that narrowed. She tried to imagine what it was. She felt something on it tickle her outer lips. Something soft like a bristle.

"Jesus, Kingsley. That's my best hairbrush. Do you know how expensive those things are?"

"Very good, *ma chérie*," he said and pulled it out of her. "Such a good hairbrush is surely washable. That is one out of five."

The next object was cold and smooth and widened as it neared the top. She remembered dinner with Kingsley last night. It had been a party with several of Kingsley's hilariously perverted friends. He'd let her have one glass of wine. Halfway through dinner he'd caught her staring at him. Winking at her, he emptied the rest of the wine bottle into his glass and raised the bottle in a toast to her.

"It's the wine bottle."

"You're a very smart little pussy, Charlie." She laughed as he pulled the bottle out of her.

She tensed a little when she felt his fingers again.

Whatever it was he was putting into her was metallic and heavy. And it was big. It had a flat bottom and grooved sides.

"Can I get a hint?" Charlotte asked.

"You'll find the answer very illuminating."

She laughed. "It's a flashlight?"

"Bien, *ma chérie*. Three out of five." He gently pulled the flashlight out of her. "The next one I'm quite certain you've had inside you before."

"Probably not. Never done the object thing."

"Are you sure about that?" Kingsley pushed her open with his fingers again. Again she felt cold, smooth metal. But this object was different. It had two parts. She heard something move like the turning of a screw and she felt her vagina start to open up.

She took a hard breath. "You have your own speculum?"

"Of course. I love to play doctor. Especially with such a beautiful and patient patient."

She waited for him to close it and pull out. But he left it in her. She heard a click. "And the flashlight will do double duty for us."

Charlotte's heart pounded. Now she *was* mortified. She knew he was looking deep inside her.

Kingsley ran his hand up her stomach and stopped at her breasts. He pinched a nipple and her body responded with a hard contraction. Kingsley laughed. She knew he had seen the muscle contraction with his own eyes.

"That is four out of five. You only have one more and you win. I'm starting to get nervous."

"I'm the one naked, spread open and being violated here," she reminded him.

"Yes, you are. Therefore I'm expecting rather gruesome revenge from you." He didn't sound the least worried about the prospect.

He closed the speculum and gently withdrew it. "Last one. If you don't get this one right, I'll be very disappointed in you, Charlie."

"Do your worst."

"I think I will."

She shivered when something soft brushed her inner thighs. She felt warm wetness again. Oh, yes, she knew what this was.

"Your tongue," she guessed, and knew she was right.

Kingsley pushed his tongue into her and

out again. He kissed her inner lips with the same passion and dexterity he used to kiss her mouth. He sucked on her clitoris, ran his tongue up and down her. For what felt like an eternity, his mouth devoured her. He pushed two fingers into her and, with both his tongue and hand working in unison, brought her to a fierce climax. Her inner muscles rippled and shivered. Her back arched. She pushed her hips up and Kingsley's fingers went deep into her. The orgasm seemed to last forever. She sank into the chair as her climax faded and left her tired and panting. Kingsley's hand was at the back of her head. He untied the blindfold and she blinked when the light intruded. Kingsley gazed at her with a dangerous grin on his lips.

"My turn," he said.

She rolled forward and went down on her knees in front of the ottoman. She unbuttoned Kingsley's pants and took him in her mouth. For such an alpha male, King didn't demand oral pleasure very often. He'd once said that if she was already on her knees, he would just fuck her doggy style and give them both a good time. She couldn't argue with that logic.

But now she could tell he was definitely in the mood.

He leaned back on his hands and tilted his hips toward her. She paused long enough to reach up and unbutton his shirt as well. Running her hands over his hard, muscled chest, she kissed his flat stomach before taking him with her mouth again. He was always so dominant, so in control of everything, that it gave her enormous satisfaction to hear him gasp and feel him flinch with the pleasure she was inflicting on him.

Kingsley reached out and slipped his fingers into her hair. He caressed the side of her face and her neck. It always amazed her how depraved he could seem one moment and how gentle and caring the next.

Charlotte took him deep in her mouth and sucked hard. She teased and caressed him with her tongue. Licked, stroked, and did everything in her power to make him moan as helplessly as he made her. Finally, Kingsley took a hard breath and came. After swallowing his semen with more pleasure than she would ever admit to, she leaned back to look at him. With his shirt pulled open all the way to his shoulders and his scarred chest and stomach on display, he was undoubtedly the most erotic man she'd ever met.

He buttoned his pants and stood up. He

took Charlotte's hand and pulled her to her feet. He kissed her long and hard. She loved that she could still taste his saltiness on her tongue.

"You won the game, Charlie. Whatever will become of me?"

"You said I get to do anything to you I want?"

"Oh, yes. Put me in a dress and take pictures. Make me walk down the street naked. Shave my testicles with a straight razor. Do you need time to decide?"

"Oh, no. I already know what I want to make you do." Charlotte wrapped her arms around Kingsley's shoulders and ran her hands through his long unruly hair.

"Charlie, no." Kingsley's voice was hard as iron.

"You don't get to say 'no' if I don't get to say 'no.' You never told me your safe word. And, need I remind you, you said I got to do anything I wanted to you. I want to cut your hair."

"I'm getting a new dragon."

"Not a chance. I'm all yours for another week...and you are getting a haircut. Stop being a coward. I'm one of the best stylists in the city."

Kingsley exhaled and shook his head. "Steele was right. You are trouble."

"He lets me cut his hair."

"He also lets you breathe fire when you're drunk. His is not an example we should be following."

Charlotte looked at Kingsley and turned the corners of her mouth down.

"*Mon Dieu*, don't pout at me. I can't resist a beautiful woman pouting. I'll have to spank you and let you cut my hair."

"Spanking later. Haircut now. We'll do it in your bathroom."

Charlotte threw on her robe and ran to her bedroom. She gathered all her supplies and took them back to Kingsley's room. Standing in the bathroom, he looked as pathetic as a child who'd lost his dog.

"Shower," she ordered.

"Only if you join me."

Charlotte sighed and pulled off her robe again. She'd probably spent as much time naked in King's house as she had clothed. Kingsley took off his shirt and pants and stepped into his large steam shower. The glass box was so full of steam she could barely see him when she entered. She laughed as he grabbed her and dragged her to him. He kissed her under the water and lifted her up. He pressed her back to the tile wall and penetrated her.

She wrapped her arms and legs around him and pushed her hips into his. She loved how strong he was, loved how easily he could lift her and take her like she weighed nothing.

He drove into her as the water poured over them. She only meant for them to get his hair wet so she could properly cut it. As she climaxed around his hard length, she decided Kingsley was definitely her favorite client of all time.

Kingsley lowered her to the floor and turned her around. He pushed into her from behind. Resting her face against the wall, she relaxed into the wet heat as he buried himself deep inside her and came again. He pulled out and Charlotte turned around.

"On your knees."

"Charlie, you devil." Kingsley dropped to the floor. He didn't seem to mind the position. Taking a fistful of shampoo she washed his hair. He kissed her stomach and hips as she lathered and rinsed his hair.

"None of that. You aren't going to fuck me until I forget what I'm doing. Up and out," she said. Kingsley stood up and left the shower.

She followed and found a towel and her robe again while Kingsley pulled on his pants without bothering to dry off. God, he looked even better wet than dry. Running out to her bedroom, she found a chair of just the right height. She brought it back, set it in the middle of the bathroom floor and pointed to it.

Kingsley sat in it with obvious reluctance. "I think I'd rather be back in *le Légion* getting shot at again."

"If you keep acting like a big baby, I will shoot you. I've never known a man so in love with his own hair before. "

"I'm in love with all of me. I'm a very lovable pervert."

"Well, you're going to be a very sexy pervert when I'm done with you. Now hold still."

She combed his hair and made a study of it. It was a good base haircut already, only too long. Clearly he hadn't gone to see his French barber in some time. She decided to cut it fairly short in the back and leave the top nice and wavy and purposefully disheveled looking.

He recoiled as she brought up her scissors.

"Big baby," she said again.

"The more you taunt me, the more you'll pay for it tomorrow."

"Your punishments are the most fun I've

had in years. You're going to have to find a better threat."

"Any suggestions?"

Charlotte thought about it. She took her first snip of his hair. It fell in a wet clump to the floor. "I guess you could kick me out earlier than we talked about."

She saw Kingsley's face in the mirror turn. The mask of the playful pervert temporarily dropped.

"I will not kick you out, Charlie. This was a business arrangement, recall? You are here to learn and then meet my client."

She continued to snip away. "I know. I'm not complaining. I've had the time of my life. I'll just, you know, miss you."

"I warned you that if you made me take my clothes off, you'd fall in love with me."

"Don't get so cocky. I'm not in love with you. I just like you. A lot."

"You know, you may like my client even more than you like me," Kingsley said.

"Is he less arrogant than you are?"

"Slightly."

"Then I probably won't."

Kingsley laughed, and she continued her work on him in silence. When she was done with the back of his hair, she moved to the front. She blocked his view of himself in the mirror as she snipped away at the sides and top of his rich brown hair. He had only a hint of a few gray hairs and no balding at all. Along with the arrogance gene, he'd gotten the great hair gene, too. She set her scissors aside and ran her hands through his hair over and over again, tousling it this way and that. She took a tiny dab of hair serum and ran it through his waves.

"Perfect." Charlotte stepped aside. She watched with anticipation as Kingsley studied himself in the mirror.

"My God," he said. "I'm even more handsome than I thought."

Charlotte slapped him on the bottom, and he pulled her into his arms. With his new cut, he looked younger and even more roguish. In fact, he looked very French. *Très* even.

"Your revenge is complete. You won the game and got to play barber."

"Stylist," she corrected. "If I beg, can I get to do one more thing tonight that you never let me do?"

"Beg away. We'll see how magnanimous I'm feeling."

"Can I sleep with you in your bed tonight?"

Kingsley sighed and kissed her on the forehead. "Charlie, while I adore hurting you, I must admit I don't actually enjoy hurting you."

"It's okay. Thought I'd ask."

"You may stay with me tonight and every night until you leave," he said.

She grinned up at him. "Really?"

"*Oui.* Now take off your clothes and get into my bed. I need to start punishing you for all your insubordination."

"Yes, sir." She took off running to the bed. Kingsley came in after her and crawled on top of her.

"Admit it," she said as he opened her robe and kissed her nipples. "You like me, too."

"I do. A good barber is so hard to find."

ON HER LAST day at Chez Kingsley, Charlotte woke up alone in his big red bed. She was surprised he was up so early, considering how late they'd stayed up playing and fucking last night.

Tired and lonely, Charlotte showered in Kingsley's bathroom and dressed. She returned to her own room and packed her things. She had a feeling she'd be back at her own apartment by tomorrow. She'd promised Kingsley she would keep an open mind about his client, whom she would meet tonight. Kingsley had told her very little about him. All she knew was that he was, as Kingsley said, "not unattractive," "wealthy," and was "longing for a deeper connection than his previous relationships." She didn't know how deeply she could connect with this guy when her heart ached at the thought of leaving Kingsley behind. But he'd trained her well. By now she was used to doing what King told her to do. She'd meet him. She'd give him a chance. And then she'd go back to her old life.

At least she'd have some spectacular memories.

At seven that evening, Kingsley came to her door. His too-handsome face wore a somber expression that pained her to see. They kissed in silence before Kingsley pulled away and whispered, "Time to go."

Offering her his arm, he escorted her to his Rolls-Royce, and she cried against his shoulder on her way to the restaurant where his client waited.

The Rolls pulled in front and parked. Charlotte wiped her face and gave King a sad smile. "I'm only doing this for you," she said.

"I know, *chérie*. But give him a chance. I think you're exactly what he's been looking for."

"Okay. I'll see you in six weeks though, right?" Charlotte straightened her hair and her dress.

He raised his eyebrow at her.

"Your next haircut," she reminded him.

He smiled. *"Bien sûr."*

Charlotte took a deep breath and walked into the restaurant. Old and elegant, it reeked of money, and she felt completely out of place. She gave her name to the maitre d', who escorted her to a private table in the corner of the restaurant. She didn't want to eat anything. She didn't even want a drink. She just wanted to run from the place and straight back into the arms of—

Staring down morosely at the floor, she saw her own face reflected back at her from a pair of riding boots polished to a mirror shine.

Charlotte looked up and smiled at Kingsley's mysterious "client."

"Bonjour, monsieur."

PULP
TIFFANY REISZ
THE ORIGINAL SINNERS
PULP LIBRARY
SAMPLER

SACRED HEART CATHOLIC CHURCH

SINNERS WELCOME

www.ingramcontent.com/pod-product-compliance
Lightning Source LLC
Chambersburg PA
CBHW030753200726
48288CB00004B/1157